"A footstool is what you need."

Kelsey laughed as she went on. "You could carry it round for your lady friends to stand on."

"That's a good idea," Bart agreed with a grin. Without warning he slid his hands beneath Kelsey's arms and lifted her into the air.

"Mr. Malone . . . Bart, put me down. What on earth . . . ?" Kelsey stopped, finding herself deposited on the hassock in front of her big armchair, her eyes now almost on a level with Bart's. "I didn't mean. . . . We aren't really . . ." she began, but stopped again, suddenly aware that Bart was going to kiss her. And suddenly aware that she was now enveloped in his arms, and he was drawing her closer until at last their lips touched. Touched very briefly, then touched and pressed together.

Katherine Arthur is full of life. She describes herself as a writer, research associate (she works with her husband, a research professor in experimental psychology), farmer, housewife, proud mother of five and a grandmother to boot. The family is definitely full of overachievers. But what she finds most interesting is the diversity of occupations the children have chosen—sports medicine, computers, finance and neuroscience (pioneering brain tissue transplants), to name a few. Why, the possibilities for story ideas are practically limitless.

Books by Katherine Arthur

HARLEQUIN ROMANCE

2755—CINDERELLA WIFE
2821—ROAD TO LOVE
2905—FORECAST OF LOVE
2948—SEND ME NO FLOWERS
2971—REMEMBER IN JAMAICA
2991—THROUGH EYES OF LOVE
3014—LOVING DECEIVER
3043—MOUNTAIN LOVESONG

ONE MORE SECRET

Katherine Arthur

Harlequin Books

TORONTO • NEW YORK • LONDON
AMSTERDAM • PARIS • SYDNEY • HAMBURG
STOCKHOLM • ATHENS • TOKYO • MILAN

Original hardcover edition published in 1990
by Mills & Boon Limited

ISBN 0-373-03061-4

Harlequin Romance first edition July 1990

SINCERELY, BART MALONE

I seem to have a mystery
I cannot solve alone.
Mr. Rocco, can you help me?
—Sincerely, Bart Malone

Sir, your story moves me.
A lady fine I know
Whose sleuthing skills can help you.
—Regards from Joe Rocco

The lady helped our hero.
A surprise he had in store.
For although he didn't know it,
Joe Rocco helped him more!

Katherine Arthur

CHAPTER ONE

'NO WONDER people can stage accidents in this place and get away with it,' Kelsey Cameron muttered to herself, staring at the five o'clock crowd of other equally confused and hungry people that ebbed and flowed in front of her, like a huge school of fish, just inside the entrance of the Big Winner supermarket. She looked at her watch. Was it worth it to plough through all that for only a bunch of bananas, a head of lettuce, and a pound of minced beef when she was already short of time? In less than two hours she was due to meet Bart Malone, general manager of the Big Winner supermarket chain, and begin playing the part of 'friend of Joe Rocco, famous detective writer'. The thought made Kelsey's nerves tingle with a combination of anxiety and excitement. Could she pull off the deception without slipping up? If she could, would she actually be able to help Bart Malone?

She took a deep breath and ran slender fingers nervously through a mop of blonde hair that perennially gave the impression that she had been caught in a high wind. Whatever the outcome, it was going to be a real adventure this time, not an imaginary one, and she had better have her wits about her. That meant no substituting a snack for a decent dinner. A small opening appeared in the surging crowd. Kelsey moved into it and began elbowing her way forward in the direction of the produce department.

'Oops! Sorry. Dreadful crowd, isn't it?' she said, flashing a wide smile as a heavy-set man looked down and glared in response to the small poke he had felt from Kelsey's elbow. He blinked, temporarily dazzled, then smiled back as she hurried past him, still smiling. There were, she thought wryly, as she pushed and smiled her way past several more people, some advantages to the fact that, in this day of working wives, almost half the shoppers were men, who responded well to her friendly smile. A disadvantage was the difficulty that even a fairly tall woman had in seeing over the strapping Californian males. Thank goodness they weren't all as tall as Bart Malone or she would feel like a small shrub in a forest of oaks!

A former college basketball star, Bart Malone was a towering man. But it was not Bart Malone's height that had most impressed Kelsey when they had met the previous week. In her normal role as a fifth-grade teacher, she had taken her class on a tour of this very store and found his quiet, gracious manner and his easy way with the children very pleasant, at least partially relieving what for Kelsey was a rather nerve-racking afternoon.

Kelsey had arrived at the store, expecting the store manager to show them around. She had certainly not expected to meet the general manager of the huge supermarket chain in person. But, Bart Malone had informed her, the store manager was ill and he had decided that it would be an interesting and useful experience for him to show a group of schoolchildren around one of his stores. They were, after all, his customers of the future. He hoped that Miss Cameron didn't mind the substitution.

It had taken Kelsey several moments of staring

dizzily into his clear grey eyes to regain her composure and say, 'Certainly not, Mr Malone. We're honoured to have you do it,' as a proper schoolteacher should. She had managed to blurt out something about recognising him as a former basketball player for UCLA to cover her confusion. The truth of the matter was that she was already acquainted with Bart through his fan letters to Joe Rocco. A quick, panicky calculation had told her that he could not possibly have yet received the letter she had sent him, but she found it very distracting to wonder what on earth he was going to think when he did. And whether, if she had met him first, she would have had the nerve to write the letter at all ...

Bart Malone was the first fan to have written to Joe Rocco about a real problem and ask what Rake Devlin might do if he were in Bart's shoes. To date, the fictional Rake, a daredevil, macho detective with an uncanny ability to find the flaws in a criminal's plan, had sleuthed his way through twelve successful novels. Bart no doubt assumed, along with the rest of the public, that Joe Rocco, Rake's creator, was as masculine as he sounded. Little did he suspect that Joe Rocco was the pseudonym of a blue-eyed blonde schoolteacher who only became a daring detective when she sat down at her typewriter.

Dear Mr Rocco,

I've written to you several times in the past to compliment you on the perspicacity of your creation, Rake Devlin. I've often wondered what I would do if I were to find myself in similar situations. Maybe I've even wished I would. However, now that I may be in one, I'm finding it nowhere near as entertaining as I thought it would be. I know you must be a very busy person, creating those thrilling stories as frequently as you do, but I was wondering if you might be able to give me a little insight as to how Rake Devlin might tackle my problem?

My problem is this: several people have been injured this past year in rather freakish accidents in some stores that my family and I own, and they have sued for large sums, claiming severe physical and emotional problems. So far, the insurance company has been able to settle out of court. I'm certainly happy to have them pay if anyone is seriously hurt due to some fault of my facilities or my employees. But I am not convinced that we were at fault, or that these were all accidents.

Perhaps I am suspicious since all of the injured persons were represented by the same lawyer, who advertises on television that he specialises in personal injury lawsuits. The insurance adjuster seems to think that it's simply the result of more people suing these days. Perhaps that is right, but the bizarre nature of the accidents makes me wonder. I could hire a private detective, but my addiction to detective fiction makes me want to at least try to look into it a bit more myself first. Unfortunately, I can't seem to get things to fall into a logical sequence as neatly as Rake Devlin would. Where should I begin and what clues should I look for? Should I question the people who were injured, the insurance company, or both?

Mr Rocco, I would really appreciate any suggestions that you could give me, but I will certainly understand if you are too busy, and I'll still be a big fan of Rake Devlin.

Sincerely,
Bart Malone

It had taken Kelsey several days to decide how to respond to Bart Malone's plea for help. She knew the simplest thing would be to write and say that Rake Devlin didn't do real detective work, but she had recently begun a book inspired by the newspaper articles she had seen about the recent rash of personal injury suits, not only at the Big Winner stores, but all over the United States. *The Case of the Crooked Claims* was her working title. As usual, before she began the book, she had talked over her hypothesis with her stepfather, and he had assured her that her idea was not beyond the realm of possibility.

Kelsey's stepfather, Donald McMurphy, had spent almost thirty years with the Los Angeles Police Department before he retired. His stories of his adventures as a detective had been the original inspiration that started Kelsey writing detective stories when she was only a teenager, and he was still her leading adviser.

'Just suppose,' she had suggested to him, 'that an insurance claims adjuster who's a compulsive gambler has gotten himself in debt to some underworld character. He finds a lawyer who is none too scrupulous, and between them they arrange to settle a couple of claims out of court and split the profits. But the underworld character gets wind of the scheme and uses his knowledge to blackmail the adjuster into keeping the game going and the money coming in. Not only that, but he can furnish the names of other debtors who would a lot rather be used in phoney accidents than be roughed up by the mobster's tough guys. Does that sound plausible?'

'It sure does,' Donald had replied. 'I had a case once where the claims adjuster and the lawyer were related and decided to get together on something like that. You might want to put some distance between the mobster and the other debtors, though. A third party to make the contacts. They're usually too smart to get real close.'

That suggestion had led Kelsey to invent Warren Wickersham III, a dissolute playboy-gambler who in time would fall prey to the charms of Rake Devlin's female accomplice, the luscious Dawn Daley. Her story was, Kelsey thought, almost identical to the ones Bart had described. She could suggest to him the ideas that had occurred to her, as long as she warned him that they were nothing more than speculations.

There had been another reason for Kelsey's reluctance to say no to Bart Malone's request for help. His earlier fan letters had indicated he paid close attention to the details of her stories and appreciated the fine points. It was hard to let down someone who took the trouble to write and compliment the author!

As a result, Kelsey sat down at her typewriter and wrote a friendly response to Bart Malone's letter, suggesting that he might look for collusion between the lawyer and the claims adjuster, along with some common element between the supposed victims, such as compulsive gambling or unsavoury associates. 'Let me know how it turns out,' she added in a handwritten postscript.

She had the letter in an envelope, when something made her stop before she added the stamp. She lived in Manhattan Beach, California. Bart Malone lived only a short distance away along the coast, in another of the lovely coastal suburbs of Los Angeles. What a shame that she couldn't just phone him. He had given Joe Rocco his telephone number. But... Kelsey sighed. There was no way. It was a secret that only her family shared and her agent had warned her to keep it that way. Besides, Bart Malone had probably built up a wonderful image of Joe Rocco as a strong, muscular, handsome, intrepid male, not unlike his fictional hero, Rake Devlin. Having him turn into a female schoolteacher might be a shock from which he'd never recover. Kelsey put the stamp on the letter, stuck it in her back pocket, and tied her running shoes on her feet.

She was jogging along the shore, with the intention of turning inland and carrying the letter to the post office, when an idea struck her. 'Why not?' she said aloud, turned round and ran home again.

I'll make sure Donald doesn't know anything terrible about the Malones, just to be on the safe side, she thought. If he didn't, she would write to Bart Malone and ask if he'd like to have some help from the woman who was the prototype for Rake Devlin's frequent accomplice and old flame, Dawn Daley. Of course, she would have to make it clear that the woman was now a schoolteacher, not someone who chased criminals all day and partied all night. But it would be so exciting to be involved, even in an advisory capacity only, in a real case that paralleled the story she was writing!

The telephone was ringing when Kelsey re-entered her apartment. 'Hello!' she said breathlessly. 'Oh, Donald! I was just going to call you. Do you know anything about the Malone family that owns the Big Winner supermarkets?'

'The Malones? Of course I know the Malones! They're a regular dynasty,' Donald replied. 'I knew old Clyde Malone when he opened his first Big Winner store back in the forties. Heaven only knows how many huge supermarkets they have now, all over the state. It's his grandson, Bartholomew—they call him Bart—who runs them now. Why are you interested in them, Kelsey? Are you thinking of teaching those schoolkids of yours about one of the great American success stories? That would be the way to do it, telling them about some real people like the Malones.'

'I might do that,' Kelsey replied, 'but it was mostly because of a letter I got. I expect you've seen in the papers that the Big Winner stores have had a lot of personal injury suits in the past year, the kind of thing I've based my new book on. And a few days ago, I got a letter from Bart Malone asking Joe Rocco what Rake Devlin would do if he suspected that the cases weren't legitimate. I was just curious about what kind of a person Bart Malone is. Do you know him?'

'I haven't really seen him often since he grew up,' Donald replied. 'Bart was a tall, skinny kid, but he's a good-looking man now. Kind of quiet, but I understand he's a real go-getter when it comes to running those stores. I was talking to his dad, Ray, just last month. We still belong to the same shooting club and have a drink together now and then. Ray says that Bart's one of those people that you call a workaholic. That accident business has got him really worried.'

Kelsey frowned. 'Did you talk to your friend Ray about the accidents?'

'A little bit. Why?'

'Oh, nothing. I just . . . well, I wondered. I was really surprised that Bart Malone would write the kind of letter that he did. You didn't let the cat out of the bag, did you?'

'Kelsey, of course not.' Donald sounded offended. 'You know I wouldn't do that. But now that you mention it . . .' he paused and cleared his throat '. . . it might be interesting if you could figure out some way to meet Bart Malone and really work on the case with him. It's a lot more exciting than just writing about it and it could make your book more realistic.'

For a moment, Kelsey stared at her telephone, dumbfounded. Could Donald be clairvoyant?

'Kelsey, are you there?' Donald asked into the silence.

'Yes, I'm here,' she answered. 'As a matter of fact, the same thing had occurred to me. I was thinking of telling Bart Malone, as Joe Rocco, of course, that the original Dawn Daley was alive and well in Manhattan Beach and she might be willing to help him. Do you think he'd go for that idea?'

'By golly, I think he might,' Donald said enthusiastically. 'That's a terrific idea, Kelsey. Like I say, I don't know Bart real well, but his dad's a fine man. Not snobbish at all, in spite of all their money. He's still the same guy he was when I went to his wedding. Always full of jokes and fun.'

'I didn't realise you knew them that well,' Kelsey said, surprised. 'How did that happen?'

'Well, you see, old Clyde's first store was on my beat back when I was a street cop. His boys Dan and Raymond both went into the business with him. I remember when Dan got his own store to manage, and then pretty soon Ray had one too. That was right after I became a detective. After I got into detective work, I didn't see as much of them any more, but,

like I said, I went to Ray's wedding, and I've known
his boys since they were little sprouts. Bart's older
brother Rutherford, they call him Ford, turned out
to be sort of a black sheep. Didn't want to go into
the business, and likes to chase the ladies. Had a few
run-ins with the law, too, but nothing serious. But
Bart's always been a straight arrow and a hard
worker. No time for foolishness. Of course, I haven't
seen him much in recent years. After all, it's been
about ten years since I retired and married your
mother.'

'Time does fly, doesn't it?' Kelsey said with a sigh.
It seemed only yesterday that an eighteen-year-old
Kelsey had watched her widowed mother marry the
handsome retired police officer. Less than a year
later, inspired by Donald's stories of his years in the
police force, she had decided to try her hand at
writing detective novels. She was out of college,
teaching, before she invented Rake Devlin and her
stories began to sell. She loved both vocations so
much that she had never wanted to abandon either,
considering the writing a bonus that enabled her to
live much more comfortably than her teacher's salary
would have done.

'I wonder why Donald called?' Kelsey mused after
he had hung up. He seldom phoned just to chat. Oh,
well. She'd probably distracted him with his
memories of the Malones. If it was anything
important, he'd call again. It was certainly good to
hear from him that Bart Malone was a good, solid
citizen, even a workaholic. She wouldn't want to get
involved in working with someone like his brother.

Kelsey read the letter from Bart once more, then
resolutely sat down at her typewriter again and wrote
him a new letter from Joe Rocco. She gave him her

ideas again, then told him that the woman who had inspired Dawn Daley's character, a woman who was really sharp at solving criminal plots, lived quite close to Bart. She still enjoyed dabbling in detective work. He (Joe) would fill her in on Bart's problem and let her know that Bart might call, but he should be warned that the woman in question, a Ms Kelsey Cameron, was now a schoolteacher and a very busy person and would not want to be bothered unless Bart seriously wanted her help. After that warning, Kelsey wrote down her telephone number and took the letter to the post office, so that it could start on its circuitous journey back to Bart. Her agent, in his almost paranoid desire to protect her secret identity, required that all mail to and from Joe Rocco be sent through his office in New York.

It was two weeks before Good Friday when Kelsey mailed the letter. It would be perfect, she thought, if Bart Malone contacted her the following week. School would be out for the Easter vacation from Good Friday until the week after Easter, a good time for them to get together and make some plans. To ensure that the letter did not get delayed at her agent's office, she rang and alerted his secretary to send it on immediately. After that, she spent extra time catching up on her school work so that, if Bart did call, she would be available. She had not counted on meeting the man in person in the meantime, on the Tuesday after she mailed her impulsive letter.

'Now he'll never call,' Kelsey told herself the night after the class tour. He would know she was nowhere near as glamorous as the Dawn Daley she portrayed and he would never believe that someone who got parsnips confused with rutabagas and dropped a ten-pound frozen turkey on his foot could be very sharp at anything! Nevertheless she was reluctant to go out in the evenings as soon as she thought Bart might have received her letter, and she made sure that her answering machine was on when she did have to leave. She calculated that the Thursday after the class tour was the first likely day for the letter to reach Bart. When he had not called by the following Monday, she was so anxious for her telephone to ring that she felt, she mused wryly, like a teenager with no date.

'Face it, Kelsey,' she told herself when, at ten p.m. the telephone still sat in sullen silence, 'he's not going to call.' She flopped down on her sofa and stared disconsolately into space. Darn the luck! She would really have liked to get to know Bart Malone and help him if she could. He seemed like such a nice person. He didn't deserve to have someone trying to defraud him with phoney accidents and false claims. He had been so polite and attentive during the tour of his store. A little quieter, more soft-spoken than most men, but she liked that. She detested men who came on strong, obviously convinced that they were doing you a big favour by noticing that you existed. Of course, Bart might be different when he was away from his stores, but from what Donald had said, he didn't spend much time away from them.

Kelsey glanced at her watch. Five minutes after ten. I could call him, she thought, then shook her head. If he wanted her help, he'd get in touch. She might as well pour herself a cup of coffee and get back to the writing she'd been neglecting the past week.

She had just filled her cup when the sudden sound of her telephone ringing in the silence startled her, so that her hand jerked and the coffee slopped over the sides. Simultaneously, she grabbed for the receiver of her kitchen wall-phone and set the cup down on the table.

'Hello!' Kelsey said breathlessly, her eyes widening as the coffee-cup teetered and then fell to the floor with a crash. 'Oh, dear,' she said.

'Ms Cameron?' enquired a deep, slightly husky voice that Kelsey recognised immediately. 'Is something wrong? This is Bart Malone calling.'

'Nothing serious,' Kelsey replied brightly. 'I just dropped my coffee-cup on the floor.' Oh, lord, that sounds stupid, she thought grimly. 'How are you, Mr Malone?'

'Very well, thanks. I've been out of town for several days, and it wasn't until today that I found I'd received a letter from Joe Rocco. I must say, I was quite surprised to hear that the same charming schoolteacher that I met only last week is an old friend of his. Why didn't you tell me? He must have contacted you before you visited the store.'

'Because it was entirely up to you if you wanted to contact me in that capacity,' Kelsey replied quickly. Of course, Bart hadn't yet said that he did. 'Do you?' she asked. 'I mean, would you like me to try to . . . to help?' Good heavens! She sounded as if her tongue had a knot in it. Not to mention her brain!

'Yes, I certainly would,' Bart replied, 'if you have the time. Of course, I wouldn't want to interfere with your—er—family plans, what with the holiday coming up and all.'

'Oh, I don't have a family,' Kelsey replied, then grimaced as she immediately realised that she had made another stupid remark. 'That is, I do have a family,' she corrected. 'My parents and a sister. But my parents live in Santa Barbara, and I only plan on visiting them over the Easter weekend. I'm free except for then.'

'That's good.' Bart sounded relieved. 'It's hard to tell these days whether Ms means a woman is single or not. So many married women are keeping their maiden names, too, that it's very confusing.'

'It certainly is,' Kelsey agreed, 'but I'm not hiding anything. I'm definitely *Miss* Kelsey Cameron.' And Mr Joe Rocco! What on earth would Bart think if he knew about that?

'Well, then, Miss Cameron, where should we begin? I'm open to your suggestions. I must admit I'm a little awed by someone of whom Joe Rocco thinks so highly.'

'Goodness, you shouldn't be,' Kelsey replied. 'I'm not a professional detective, although I know a good one I can consult if necessary. I'm just a person who loves to try to solve mysteries, and it sounds as though you have one worth looking into. Has anything new happened on your case?'

'I'm afraid so,' Bart Malone replied, his voice grating with aggravation. 'There's been another accident.'

'Oh, no!' Kelsey said, frowning. 'What happened this time? Was it another odd one?'

'Extremely,' was the answer. 'A fellow named Santos lost the little finger of his left hand in the conveyor belt at the check out counter when it got caught between the moving and stationary parts. I'm still not clear exactly how it happened. All that I am sure of is that the lawyer is once again the same, and this time the claim is much bigger. We're supposed to believe that the man suffered such an extreme emotional trauma that he'll never work again.'

'That's ridiculous!' Kelsey exclaimed quickly.

'That's what I said,' Bart agreed. 'I don't like to sound hard-hearted, but I really resent someone trying to live off us for the rest of his life when I'm still not sure that it wasn't at least partly the man's own fault that he was injured. It's not as if the fellow were a concert pianist. He's a bulldozer operator. I know I'd expect to go on working if I lost a finger. Even an entire hand.'

'I don't think you sound hard-hearted at all. I can't imagine that it wasn't the man's fault to some extent,' Kelsey said sympathetically. Bart Malone sounded as if his patience was wearing very thin, and she did not blame him at all. 'I've never yet seen a checkout counter that would reach up and grab someone's hand. The man must have done something really stupid, and now he's expecting you and your insurance company to compensate him for his mistake. That's not fair at all.'

Bart chuckled. 'That sounds exactly like the kind of woman Joe Rocco would recommend. There must be quite an *alter ego* hidden inside that proper schoolteacher that I met.'

Kelsey almost dropped the telephone. 'Yes, I suppose you could say that,' she said weakly, 'but I'm not really much like Dawn Daley, as you must have noticed.'

'And I'm not much like Rake Devlin,' Bart replied, 'but I'll give it a try. I suppose we should get together and go over the information that I have.'

'Yes, that would be a good idea,' Kelsey said, wondering to what extent Bart Malone intended to take on the role of her overwhelmingly aggressive detective. 'How would Thursday night at my apartment be for you? After that it's the Easter vacation and I won't have anything to distract me except some papers to grade for ten whole days.'

'That sounds excellent. I'll put all my information together by then,' Bart said. 'I'm really looking forward to seeing you again. I'd intended to call you in any case, and find out how the tour of the store went over with your students.'

'Oh, it went over very well,' Kelsey replied. 'They learnt a lot. And I—I was very impressed with the way you talked *to* them instead of talking down to them. So many people don't realise how much fifth graders can understand.'

'Why, thank you.' Bart's deep voice had a smile in it. 'That's nice to hear. Until Thursday, then.'

Kelsey hung up the phone, feeling slightly dazed. Bart Malone had been going to call her in any case. Of course, it was probably only to find out about the tour, so that he would know if he needed to do anything differently in the future. Lots of classes must tour his stores, and he was the kind of person who liked to do things well. It didn't mean anything special. Or did it? And what did she care if it did? She was only interested in his mysterious rash of accidents.

Tuesday and Wednesday dragged by. Kelsey tried to tell herself that it was only the usual state of pre-vacation restlessness that invaded her students, rubbing off on her. There was no doubt that she felt a little *frisson* of excitement every time she thought of seeing Bart Malone again, but she put it down to the fact that she was nervous about playing a role with him, instead of just being her usual self.

When the final bell rang on Thursday, she dashed out of the door immediately after her class, anxious to get home and make her apartment spotless before Bart's arrival that evening. As usual, that task took longer than Kelsey expected. Now, with the long queues at the supermarket, she was going to have to fly in order to finish her dinner and still have time to make herself look her best. Her typically casual, California-style outfit of blue jeans, high-heeled sandals, and a printed T-shirt that stated 'I'm Not the Teacher's Pet, I'm the Teacher', which her sister had given her, was definitely not what she planned to be wearing when Bart Malone arrived.

Kelsey finally cleared the bottleneck of people crowded round the cashier's booth and shifted into high gear, her high heels clicking along briskly as she passed the corner bin of oranges and entered the produce area of the huge supermarket. Straight ahead, bunches of bananas were displayed on hooks attached to an artificial palm tree. Cute idea, Kelsey thought, moving swiftly forwards, her gaze intent on a nicely yellowed bunch of bananas slightly above her eye level. Just as she reached for it, her heel skidded crazily sideways on something slippery. At the same moment as she felt her balance going, she saw another hand extended towards the same bunch. 'Whoops!' she cried, grabbing for the hand.

While Kelsey's feet continued their slide, she caught the hand, large and male, which had grasped the bunch of yellow fruit, which still clung to the hook on the plastic tree. Her feet struck the base of the tree, turning it into a falling missile which pursued Kelsey and the owner of the large male hand to the hard, tiled floor of the produce department. Stars danced briefly before Kelsey's eyes as her head bumped against the floor, aided both by whiplash and the combined weight of the male person and the banana tree on top of her. A suntanned face with a lock of soft dark hair falling across the forehead loomed above Kelsey's. A festoon of bananas was draped over one of the man's broad shoulders. Clear grey eyes peered anxiously into hers.

'Oh, lord, Miss Cameron. I can't believe this,' said a deep, worried voice. 'This is terrible. I know you can't be one of them. Are you all right?'

'Believe what? One of whom?' Kelsey felt as if the world were revolving around her like a catherine wheel. She stared back into those remarkably clear eyes and tried to remember how on earth she had got into this position and where she had seen those eyes before. She could scarcely breathe from the weight on her chest.

'What's so terrible? Are there aliens coming?' she demanded, her breath coming in hoarse gasps. All that she could think of was that somehow, when she had touched the banana tree, it had come to life and transported her to some strange, new land, where Prince Charming, or a reasonable facsimile, had fallen from its plastic fronds and landed practically on top of her. 'Where am I?' she faltered.

The grey eyes clouded over, and the man leaned back, almost knocking over an aproned clerk as he flung the banana tree off them and leapt out of Kelsey's field of view. 'She's hurt! It looks like a concussion. Call an ambulance,' she heard him bark at the clerk, who was now clutching the plastic tree and attempting to right it. 'And hurry it up!' he added when the clerk did not move immediately.

As soon as the weight was removed from her chest and she could breathe again, Kelsey's vision began to clear. She stared at the man who was barking out orders. It was Bart Malone! Good heavens. The poor man thought she was another victim of his rash of accidents! She started to push herself to a sitting position. 'I don't need an ambulance, I'm . . .' she began.

'Don't move!' Bart Malone ordered, immediately crouching beside her. He removed his jacket, folded it, and carefully laid it behind her head. 'Please, Miss Cameron,' he said more softly, 'lie down until the ambulance gets here.' He peered into her eyes, his forehead furrowed anxiously.

'But I'm all right, Mr Malone. Really,' Kelsey said, without much conviction. She was once again entranced by those grey eyes, now only a foot or so from her own. They looked pussy-willow soft with worry, their dark fringes startling by contrast. Dark brows frowned with an artistic sweep above an arrow-straight nose. Her initial impression that Prince Charming had fallen with her was not too far off the mark. Bart's shoulders were so broad that they filled most of her field of view, and the light shining from behind him made golden highlights gleam in his dark hair. Bart Malone would do for almost any girl's prince. 'I don't want to go to the hospital,' she said sulkily. 'I'll miss our appointment.'

'I'm afraid I'll have to insist,' was the firm reply.

'But you know I'm not going to sue you,' Kelsey protested, frowning. 'Please . . .' She tried to raise herself, but Bart firmly held her by her shoulders.

'Just stay put,' he said. 'The ambulance should be here in a minute.'

'You're stubborn,' Kelsey complained.

'Very,' Bart agreed. A little twinkle sent silver sparks flying in his eyes. 'I'm famous for it.'

'So am I,' Kelsey said, 'and I don't want to go to the hospital. I hate hospitals.' Her head was beginning to clear now, and she hated the feeling of being helpless, and the strange looks she was getting from the little crowd of interested onlookers who had gathered. It would be different if she were really trying to appear injured so that she could sue . . .

Like a light flashing on, a new thought occurred to Kelsey. 'Mr Malone,' she whispered, beckoning for him to bend closer.

'What is it?' he asked, looking more worried again.

'I just had a great idea,' she replied in an even softer whisper. 'This may be the perfect way to find out some things about your accident victims. I'm sure I'm all right, but I could make a big fuss and pretend I'm not, and go on to the hospital and see if anyone turns up to encourage me to sue you.'

Bart Malone stared at Kelsey, the changing lights in his eyes mirroring his conflicting responses to her suggestion. 'I don't think that would be a good idea, Miss Cameron,' he said finally. 'It might be dangerous. I want your advice, but I certainly don't want to endanger you in any way. Besides, I'm afraid you may really be injured. You'd better go on to the hospital and have a thorough check-up. I'll come along and make sure . . .'

'Don't do that,' Kelsey pleaded. 'I'm really quite capable of taking care of myself. I do it all the time. I won't find out anything useful if you come along.' She looked at Bart hopefully, at the same time wishing fervently that he wouldn't look so anxious. He must think she was made of glass. 'I'm going to start pretending now,' she whispered, 'just in case someone is watching.' She started to push herself upwards, then clasped a hand to her forehead, groaned loudly, and lay back down.

Bart looked startled, but he managed to keep his face almost impassive, his next words showing that he would follow her suggestion and was quite adept at playing the game. 'I think I hear the ambulance coming, Miss . . .' He raised his eyebrows questioningly.

'Cameron,' Kelsey replied. 'Kelsey Cameron.'

'Miss Cameron,' Bart repeated in normal tones. 'Please rest assured that Big Winner stores will see that any expenses for your care are completely covered.'

Kelsey scowled and rolled her eyes to look around at the faces of the crowd above her, still peering curiously at her prostrate form. 'They'd better be,' she said belligerently. 'It sure wasn't my fault you had something slippery on your floor.'

'We are very sincerely sorry about that,' said Bart, standing up and moving aside as the ambulance attendants appeared, carrying their portable stretcher.

Research on traumatic injuries for her novels made it quite easy for Kelsey to persuade the ambulance attendants that she had a possible concussion and neck injury. They loaded her carefully on to the stretcher and carried her to the waiting ambulance, with Bart Malone hovering nearby, looking convincingly worried. She was afraid that he might actually be worried, when he bent over the stretcher and again offered to travel in the ambulance to the hospital.

'No, thanks,' she growled, frowning at him so severely that he straightened and drew back. 'Why don't you do something useful and see that your floor gets cleaned up before someone else gets hurt? Or, if you really want to do something for me, go and feed my cat. He's going to think I've deserted him.'

'I'd be happy to, Miss Cameron, but I don't know

where you live,' Bart replied, looking relieved that she had suggested something for him to do. 'You must have a car here, too, I suppose.'

'Of course I do.' Kelsey snapped, trying hard to keep looking cross, while at the same time she was relieved that her car would be looked after. It was an elderly Porsche that she had bought second-hand, but it was still a fine car. She paused, clutched at her forehead and groaned for effect. 'Lord, but I feel sick,' she moaned. Then she glowered at poor Bart Malone again, gave him her address, and ordered him to get her key from her bag.

When he had gone, and she was safely tucked inside the moving ambulance, one of the attendants shook his head and laughed softly. 'Lady,' he said, 'you sure must not know who that guy was, the way you were ordering him around.'

'Oh? Is he somebody special?' Kelsey asked innocently.

'Only one of the richest men in Los Angeles,' the attendant replied. 'He's Bart Malone, and his family *owns* the Big Winner supermarkets. You ought to be thinking about suing them, the shape you're in. They've had a lot of suits lately, and from what I've heard it's an almost sure thing if you get the right lawyer.'

'Do you really think so?' Kelsey asked, groaning and clutching her head again to cover a sudden impulse to sit up and ask the attendant exactly what he had heard. It was, she thought, rather different actually being involved in detective work from only writing about it. She would have to keep her wits about her and make sure that she heard everything that any other accident victims would have heard and more, without appearing suspiciously curious.

'The guy hasn't lost one yet,' the attendant replied with an air that was obviously calculated to convey the idea that he was in possession of superior knowledge. He bent over Kelsey and lowered his voice. 'If you're interested in suing, I know the lawyer personally. Want me to send him around to see you?'

Kelsey eyed the man suspiciously. 'Maybe,' she said. 'But how do I know he's as good as you say?'

'He's helped a lot of other people just like you,' the man replied. 'Those big guys always end up paying when Morris Carter gets on their case.'

'Morris Carter? Haven't I seen him on TV?' Kelsey asked. He must be the lawyer that Bart had mentioned, who had represented all the other plaintiffs.

'He's the one,' the attendant replied.

'Then I'll know where to find him if I decide to sue,' Kelsey said.

'They'll probably keep you overnight,' the attendant said. 'I can tell him to stop by and see you in the morning.'

Kelsey frowned. 'No, thanks. If I want to sue, I'll go and see him. I don't want anyone bothering me until I'm ready.' The less eager she appeared, she thought, the more likely she was to hear all the arguments in favour of suing.

'But the sooner you start, the sooner . . .'

'Will you just drop it?' Kelsey snapped. 'If I want to sue, I'll sue. If I don't, I won't!' She gave a quite sincere moan after that outburst, for her head really did hurt.

'Feisty dame, aren't you?' said the attendant with a chuckle. 'OK, Miss Cameron. But I'll give your name to Morris, just in case. I think you'll be looking for him soon enough. I mean, what's the point in passing up something that's like a lottery ticket on a sure thing?'

Kelsey closed her eyes and said nothing more, but the attendant's words gave her plenty of food for thought. It definitely appeared that there was something going on that was well past the point of legal lawsuits. The attendant might even be getting a small pay-off for encouraging accident victims to sue. It would be interesting to see how the lawyer tried to persuade her. Would he too mention some 'guarantee' based on past performance? Or would he try to stay within legal boundaries, and leave the heavy-handed persuasion to someone else?

The ambulance arrived at the Casualty entrance, and Kelsey was quickly wheeled into one of the emergency rooms and transferred to a bed, where huge overhead lights and an intimidating array of high-tech instruments aided a bevy of doctors and technicians, who inspected her thoroughly from head to toe and then sent her on to the X-ray unit. All their efforts uncovered nothing more serious than a mild concussion and a slightly wrenched neck. She was fitted with a foam neck-brace and, as the ambulance attendant had predicted, assigned to a private room for the night.

'But there's nothing wrong with me. I want to go home,' Kelsey complained. It seemed unlikely that suffering a dinner of hospital food and then sleeping in an uncomfortable bed would further her investigation.

'Now, don't you fuss,' said the cheerful young nurse who had accompanied her to the room and helped put her to bed. 'We want to be absolutely sure that no other symptoms are going to show up before we send you home. Mr Malone is having a special dinner sent in for you, and you can just relax and watch the television and pretend you're in a fine hotel.'

'Hmph,' Kelsey said, remembering to act her part. 'He must be afraid that I'll sue him. I did have a nasty fall because of something slippery on the floor at one of his stores.'

The nurse looked at Kelsey knowingly. 'Another customer for that sleazy Morris Carter?' she asked. 'I'll bet that guy is really raking in the millions.'

'I might sue,' Kelsey replied with a shrug, 'but I doubt it. I expect I'll be fine before the Easter vacation is over.'

'You must be a teacher,' the nurse commented. 'No one else gets an Easter vacation. Me, I have to find someone to take care of my kids.'

'I'm sure that is a problem,' Kelsey said, trying to sound sympathetic. Privately, she was very glad that some twenty-two sets of parents were going to be entertaining her charges for the next week and a half. She loved them dearly, but needed a break now and then.

The nurse nodded, then gave Kelsey a smile. 'It is, but I wouldn't trade jobs with you for the world. Of course, we're both underpaid. If I had a chance to sue someone, I'd take it in a flash.'

'It seems that everyone would these days,' Kelsey replied.

There was a knock at the door. 'Here comes your dinner,' said the nurse. Kelsey carefully turned her head to watch in amazement as an aide wheeled in a trolley laden with an elegant dinner of prime beef, baked potato, fresh broccoli with hollandaise sauce, an artichoke salad, and, for dessert, chocolate mousse.

'Good heavens,' Kelsey said, raising herself on her elbow and looking hungrily at the repast. With the trip to the hospital and all the excitement, she had lost track of time, but her stomach was suddenly, actively aware that dinner was late.

'It does look as if Mr Malone wants to get on your good side,' the nurse said drily, taking an envelope from the trolley and handing it to Kelsey. 'If our patients ate like this all the time, they'd never go home.'

'I can believe that,' Kelsey agreed, thinking of the meagre repast that she had been planning. She opened the envelope and took out a card decorated with delicate pressed flowers. Inside, scrawled in a masculine hand, was written:

My dear Miss Cameron,
    I am so very sorry that you were injured today. I hope that having a good dinner will make your brief stay in the hospital more bearable. Please accept my most heartfelt apologies and wishes for your speedy recovery.
Sincerely,
Bart Malone

Kelsey smiled to herself. Bart Malone was being very good about sticking to their little deception. He had been careful not to say anything that would indicate they were connected in any way. And it was very sweet of him to send her such a lovely dinner. As soon as the nurse was gone, she made herself as comfortable as a person wearing a hospital gown and sitting on the edge of the bed could be, and began eating. She was contemplating removing the uncomfortable neck-brace, which seemed to poke her when she swallowed, when there was a knock on the door.

'Come in,' she called. The procession that entered made her put down her fork and stare.

'More goodies from Mr Malone,' said the nurse, entering with a large floral arrangement in her hands. She made a face and gestured behind her. 'I'm not sure whoever took his order got it quite right.' Following her was another nurse with a bunch of shiny helium balloons, each a different colour, and, last of all, a young nurse's aide carrying a huge, white, stuffed plush rabbit with a pink bow around his neck. While the nurses put the flowers and balloons where Kelsey could see them, the aide held up the rabbit as if it were a small child.

'Where would you like this Easter bunny?' she asked. 'Do you want it in bed with you? It's very cuddly.'

'I . . . guess that would be all right,' Kelsey replied, watching silently, as the rabbit was placed beside her and the nurses again left the room. She could see why the nurse thought the gifts strange, but they were not to someone who read the Rake Devlin series. It was obvious that Bart was playing the role of Rake Devlin to her Dawn Daley to the hilt. One of the reasons why the dashing Rake Devlin had made such a hit with that sentimental lady of fiction was that he often sent her whimsical gifts of stuffed animals and balloons and other toys. It was an idea borrowed from Kelsey's past, from that time long ago . . .

Kelsey shook her head and slowly tried to finish her dinner, glancing from time to time at the rabbit, and trying to ignore the deep ache that had invaded her heart. At last, she pushed the tray away, sat back on her bed and picked up the rabbit. It had been a long, long time since anyone had bought her a

stuffed toy. Once, there had been a boy named Tom,
who bought her so many that they covered the bed
in her college room. A boy named Tom, handsome
and wild and adventurous but, underneath, a kind,
gentle person who made her feel so loved, so very
special. Whose life had been snuffed out by a
drunken fool, on a foggy, lonely road . . .

'Forget it,' Kelsey scolded herself, blinking back
the tears that came with the memory. 'That was seven
years ago.' She held the rabbit up in front of her and
looked into its glassy, smoke-coloured eyes. It had a
slightly worried look. Kelsey hugged the rabbit
experimentally and then shook her head. If anyone
were to look into her room and see her, they would
think she was crazy, just as they would probably
think Bart Malone was, if they believed he had
actually bought the rabbit. A mistaken order, the
nurse thought, but Kelsey doubted it. However . . .

'I wonder if Bart Malone would have thought of it
on his own?' she mused aloud. What kind of man
was he, really? Polite and soft-spoken, except when
giving emergency orders, very thoughtful, decisive,
clever and adept at going along with her little ruse.
Very nice-looking. A Joe Rocco fan. A very
favourable report, so far. Kelsey sighed, then
adjusted her bed and leaned back with the rabbit still
in the crook of her arm.

All Bart Malone knew about her so far was that
she was a very clumsy schoolteacher who broke
coffee-cups and fell down under banana trees, and
who stubbornly insisted on carrying out her idea to
go to the hospital as a victim who might possibly sue
him. She was going to have to improve her image
tomorrow. Maybe she should really sue . . . but she'd
have to talk that over with Bart first. And she couldn't

pretend to be really immobilised because she had to go back to teaching a week from Monday . . .

'Oh, to heck with it,' Kelsey said, snuggling the rabbit against her and reaching for the television remote control. 'I'll figure it out tomorrow.' She flipped on the TV and stared at the gyrating image of a group of dancers. Her head still ached, and her vision was a little fuzzy. The dancers seemed to be forming into circles that looked like two, huge grey eyes. It was probably those painkillers which they had given her. Maybe if she closed her eyes for just a minute . . .

CHAPTER TWO

'WELL, well. Lucky rabbit. I guess anything is better than sleeping alone, is it, Ms Cameron?' Kelsey opened her eyes to see a new, young doctor standing beside her bed, a knowing smile quirking one corner of his mouth. 'And how did we sleep last night?' the doctor asked.

'*We* slept just fine,' Kelsey replied coldly. She was somewhat embarrassed to be discovered clutching a stuffed rabbit while she slept, but the doctor's sarcasm annoyed her. Instead of putting the rabbit down, she continued to hold it tightly. 'When can *we* go home?' she asked.

'If all of your signs are normal, as soon as you'd like,' the doctor replied. 'If you could just put that rabbit aside for a moment . . .'

Kelsey did so with exaggerated reluctance. A few minutes later, the doctor reported that she was free to go.

'I'd be glad to take your rabbit's place any night I'm not on duty,' he said with a sly grin.

'Thanks, but he and I are going steady,' Kelsey said sweetly. As soon as the doctor left, she dressed quickly. 'What do I have to do to check out of the hospital?' she asked the nurse who was now on duty.

'Not a thing,' the nurse replied. 'A Mr Malone has taken care of everything for you, and he left a number for you to call when you needed transportation home.'

Kelsey called the number, and was told that a car

would be at the hospital door in fifteen minutes. According to regulations, she had to be taken to the door in a wheelchair. Wearing her neck-brace, with the rabbit on her lap, one nurse pushing the chair and another nurse following with her balloons and flowers, she started for the main entrance of the hospital. She was being wheeled across the lobby when a dapper man, wearing a dark grey suit and carrying a briefcase, approached her.

'Miss Cameron?' he asked, coming to her side and walking beside her.

'That's right,' she replied, giving the man a cool glance out of the corners of her eyes. He looked pale without his television make-up, but was obviously Morris Carter. 'And you are?'

'Morris Carter, Miss Cameron,' he replied. 'I'm certainly glad to see that you're being released already. How are you feeling this morning? I understand you had a nasty fall yesterday at the Big Winner supermarket in Manhattan Beach.'

'I'm feeling much better, thank you,' Kelsey replied, deliberately avoiding eye contact with the man for fear her contempt for him would be only too obvious. Wearing the neck-brace made it easy, for she simply pretended that she could not turn her head and kept looking straight ahead.

'Good, good,' Morris Carter said with false joviality. 'Now, I know you probably expect to recover completely in a short time, and you're not the kind of a person to complain, even if you keep having headaches and your neck hurts a little, but I'd like to suggest to you that you ought to keep your options open for a while, just in case things don't go as well as you expect. As you may have noticed on your television, I specialise in personal injury suits.

I'm especially interested in those cases where the injured party is clearly not at fault and those responsible for the accident should be made to bring their operations up to scratch so that others won't be injured in the future. I think of it as my own small contribution to making the world a safer and better place for everyone.'

'How do you know I'm not at fault?' Kelsey asked. 'You weren't there.'

'Well, of course I don't know that,' Morris Carter said smoothly, 'but I think it's safe to assume that an intelligent young woman like yourself was not behaving in such a manner as to cause herself to land flat on her back, thereby inflicting considerable pain and suffering on herself.' He hurried ahead and stopped on the pavement, as the nurse wheeled Kelsey through the automatic doors. 'I can see that your boyfriend was quite worried about you,' he said, gesturing towards Kelsey's assorted gifts. 'I'm sure that he feels that you deserve some compensation for your suffering.'

'Possibly,' Kelsey said, giving Morris Carter a quick look.

'Well, you take your time and think about it. Talk it over with your boyfriend,' said Morris Carter, handing Kelsey a business card. 'I'll be looking forward to hearing from you. In the meantime, I'd like to give you one bit of free advice.' He bent in front of Kelsey and gave her an oily smile. 'Don't sign anything absolving Big Winner of any further responsibility. If you do that, I won't be able to help you, unless, of course, you sign it under duress.'

'Duress?' Kelsey raised her eyebrows and gave Morris Carter an innocent stare.

'Bart Malone has been known to get pretty rough.'

Morris said, his eyes narrowed meaningfully. 'I'd stay away from him if I were you.'

'I certainly will,' Kelsey replied. She smiled suddenly. 'Unless, of course, I decide to marry him instead,' she added.

The confusion on Morris Carter's face at the sound of Kelsey's words was monumental. She could barely keep from bursting out laughing, in spite of the fact that at the same moment she was cursing herself for having said something so outrageous. Why on earth had that notion popped into her head and out of her mouth with such unpremeditated aplomb? It was like the things that happened when she was writing one of her novels. All of a sudden, Rake Devlin would do something she hadn't planned at all, and it would turn out, in the end, to have been exactly the right thing.

Kelsey hoped fervently that this was another case like that, for, while she was talking to Morris, a limousine had pulled up at the kerb and a uniformed chauffeur had got out, waiting politely nearby for her to finish her conversation. The chauffeur had doubtless heard what both she and Morris said, although his face was the epitome of well-trained impassivity. She was sure, however, that he was neither deaf nor dumb, and that word would get back to Bart Malone. She only hoped she would be able to talk to Bart first. Otherwise, he might think that Kelsey Cameron was just another little gold-digger, anxious to cash in on her acquaintance with Bart in the most profitable way possible.

The chauffeur, a middle-aged man who informed Kelsey that his name was Henry, drove her to her apartment, so swiftly that she wondered if he had done his apprenticeship as an ambulance driver.

'Your automobile is in your garage, miss,' he told her, as helped carry in her balloons and flowers. 'And I believe Mr Malone fed your cat already this morning.'

'How kind of him,' Kelsey said. 'I'm sure Devil appreciated it.' The chauffeur stood, or rather hovered, near the door after he had deposited Kelsey's flowers on top of a bookcase. 'Is there anything else, Henry?' Kelsey asked, sensing his discomfort and wondering if he wanted to say something about her sudden threat to marry his employer.

Henry cleared his throat. 'Is it true that you are a good friend of Joe Rocco's?' he asked.

'Oh, yes,' Kelsey replied, not sure whether to feel relieved, or surprised that Bart had told him who she was. 'He and I are the best of friends. I've known him all my life.'

'Well . . .' Henry looked down shyly, then gathered his courage and looked at Kelsey. 'Do you suppose, Miss Cameron, that if I were to send some of my copies of his books to him, and included the necessary postage, he would autograph them for me and send them back? He is my favourite author.'

Kelsey almost ran to the man and hugged him. This was the first time that she had encountered, in person, a fan's adulation. She managed to restrain herself and only smile broadly. 'I know Joe would be delighted to do that,' she replied. 'He's really a very nice man.'

'I'm sure he must be,' Henry said, returning Kelsey's smile. 'Thank you, Miss Cameron.'

'You're welcome,' Kelsey replied. As Henry turned to leave, she decided that this would be the time to scotch any ideas he might be brewing from her impulsive statement that she might marry Bart Malone. 'By the way, Henry,' she said, 'I only said that I might marry Mr Malone in order to shake up Morris Carter. If you remember, Rake Devlin has a theory that getting people's thinking muddled up can lead them to make mistakes.'

Henry frowned. 'I'm sure that's an excellent move, Miss Cameron,' he said, 'but I do think you should consider marrying Mr Malone in any case. I think that would be an excellent idea, for both of you.' After giving that unexpected piece of advice, he managed to nod and appear politely deferential before he went out and closed the door behind him.

'Well, for goodness' sake,' Kelsey said, staring after him. She had read of English butlers who meddled unrepentantly in their employers' affairs, but, having had little contact with servants of any kind, had always assumed that they were more fiction than fact. Now, here was the first chauffeur she had ever met, doing exactly that!

'I wonder how Mr Malone likes that sort of thing,' she said to Devil. Perhaps he didn't mind, for apparently he had confided in Henry about her role in the lawsuit investigation. The large black cat was sniffing suspiciously at the white rabbit, which Kelsey had set on her sofa, fixing her with a thoughtful, green-eyed stare. Then he curled up next to the rabbit, purring loudly. Kelsey smiled to herself at the incongruous pair. 'I've got to get a picture of that,' she said, 'as soon as I get this blasted neck-brace off.' She was just reaching for the velcro tab on the neck-brace when there was a knock on the door. She pushed the tab down firmly and went to answer. There stood Henry again, hat in hand.

'I'd just started off when I got a call from Mr

Malone,' he said. 'He asked me to tell you that he will be by to see you at noon, and will bring luncheon with him.'

Kelsey opened her mouth, meaning to say that she would prefer Bart Malone to ask rather than announce, but the pleased look on Henry's face stopped her. She could tell that he was glad to be the bearer of such news, and would be very unhappy if she grumbled about Mr Malone's presumption. Instead, she only closed her mouth again and nodded. 'Thank you, Henry,' she said. 'I'll be expecting him.'

When Henry had left, Kelsey was finally able to remove the annoying neck-brace. She rolled her head round experimentally and found that, as far as she could tell, her neck was as good as ever. The brace was so uncomfortable that she had begun to wonder if it was.

'Thank goodness I already have this place cleaned up,' Kelsey said, surveying the comfortable clutter of her pleasant living-dining-room, with its oak-framed upholstered furniture and round oak table, the usual piles of books and magazines on every available surface. Bart Malone, Kelsey thought, was doubtless used to something a lot more elegant, maintained to perfection by a staff of servants. Oh, well. As far as he knew, she was only a schoolteacher on a limited budget, and there was nothing in her apartment to tell him otherwise. She kept everything associated with her successful writing career locked tightly away in filing cabinets. The few expensive outfits she had bought were enclosed in garment bags in her wardrobe. The little back bedroom that she used as a study looked only like a room where a teacher planned her lessons and marked her papers. Bart might have been surprised to find that she drove an elderly green Porsche, but he probably assumed that it was a bargain she had got through some relative or friend.

Kelsey spent what remained of the morning giving herself and her hair a thorough cleaning, for it seemed to her that an aura from the hospital clung to her entire body. When there was a knock on her door promptly at twelve noon, Kelsey was ready, wearing a pink silk shirt and ivory-coloured jeans which she hoped had the right air of casual chic for the occasion. She glanced out of her window. Parked in front of her apartment were both an unfamiliar black Mercedes and a white delivery van with the words 'Pierre's Romantic Catering—Gourmet Delights for that Special Tête-àTête' inscribed on the side.

Good heavens, now what? *Filet mignon* for lunch? Was Bart Malone determined to fatten her up? Kelsey wondered, grabbing her neck-brace and fastening it quickly. She had decided she would continue to wear it in public as long as there was any chance that she might want to use her supposed injuries as a tool in the investigation. Having food delivered was not exactly public, but if the ambulance attendant could be in league with Morris Carter, why not the deliveryman from Pierre's? The brace in place, she opened her door and found herself looking up at Bart Malone, who was so tall that he would have to duck his head to go through her door.

'Good afternoon, Miss Cameron,' he said, smiling warmly at her.

'Hello, Mr Malone,' Kelsey said, vacantly contemplating the fact that his eyes were even more clear and direct than she remembered, and his wide, gentle mouth with the full lower lip was much more entrancing curving upwards than when it was downturned with worry.

'May I come in?' Bart said at last, and Kelsey realised that she had been staring, speechless, at him for some time.

'Of course!' she blurted, her cheeks suddenly feeling unusually warm. 'I'm sorry. It's just that you're . . . a lot taller than I remembered.'

Bart looked surprised, then nodded. 'That's probably because I don't seem so tall in a place with high ceilings. And, of course, yesterday you were lying down the whole time.'

Kelsey saw the deliveryman, who had followed Bart with a covered tray, give her a knowing look. Good lord, the man thought . . . 'That wasn't my idea,' she said coldly, trying to undo the false impression. She realised that it was no use, when the deliveryman grinned at her and winked.

'Where shall I put this, ma'am?' he asked politely.

'Oh, just . . . on the table. Where else?' she said, feeling more uncomfortable by the minute.

The deliveryman shrugged and placed the items from the tray on the table. 'People eat in all kinds of places,' he replied cryptically, giving Kelsey another sidelong look.

'Well, I had my last meal in the hospital,' Kelsey snapped. As the man finished his work and departed, she frowned at Bart. 'Do you realise what that man thought after you said I was lying down the whole time we were together yesterday?' she asked.

'I suppose he might have gotten the wrong impression,' Bart replied, imperturbably picking up the bottle of wine the man had brought and starting to open it.

Kelsey stared at him, her hands on her hips. 'Well, maybe you don't care,' she said, 'but I do. Or is it just that you're pretending to be Rake Devlin?'

Bart looked at Kelsey, his eyes twinkling mischievously. 'Maybe I am, or maybe I just don't pay much attention to what other people think. Now, you and I know what happened and what didn't happen. What else is there to worry about?'

'Potentially, quite a lot,' Kelsey replied. 'Suppose that I were really suing you . . .'

'Let's not get into that yet,' Bart interrupted. 'We wouldn't want our lunch to get cold. Do come and sit down.' He held out a chair for Kelsey.

'It . . . looks delicious,' Kelsey said, realising that in her distress she was appearing very ungracious. 'And the dinner last night was wonderful,' she added, as she took her seat. 'Thank you very much. I really was dreading the hospital food.'

'I'm glad to hear that,' Bart replied, helping Kelsey to move her chair into position. 'I mean, that you had a good dinner. This catering business is something I've just gotten into. I bought them out last winter, but this is the first chance I've had to check it out personally.' He put his hands on Kelsey's shoulders and bent his head down next to hers. 'I'm no Rake Devlin. And I'm certainly not going to pretend to be, except for trying to solve my problem.'

Kelsey turned her head and found her cheek against Bart Malone's. It felt cool and smooth, and he smelled of something spicy and nice. A quotation from one of her novels flitted through her mind: 'Rake liked the way her cheek felt, smooth and round, like a ripe peach. There were other things about Dawn that were ripe, too.' The knowledge of what followed that made Kelsey feel a little dizzy, and she quickly turned her head away again.

'I'm—er—glad to hear that, Mr Malone,' she said, trying to calm a feeling of near-panic. 'I mean, there's no way on earth that I can turn into a Dawn Daley. I'm just a grade-school teacher, moonlighting as a detective's helper. That's all. Don't you think maybe you'd better sit down before the onion soup gets cold?' She heard a rather disconcerting chuckle before Bart squeezed her shoulders and moved to take his place next to her.

'I do think, though,' he said as he poured them each a glass of wine, 'that it might help to get at least part-way into the character. Being adept at managing a business is quite different from being able to come up with a quick and clever story in order to find out what people are really up to.'

'I'm not sure that's the way it works,' Kelsey said. She paused and removed her neck-brace once again. 'Horrible thing,' she said, laying it aside. 'Hot as a fur piece.' She took a spoonful of her soup. 'Ummm. This is delicious. Now, as I was saying, the stories Rake Devlin uses are always based on his idea of what he needs to know, and I think real detectives work that way, too. My stepfather, Donald McMurphy, has told me a lot of stories about his days as a detective for LAPD. I believe you've met Donald. He knows your father well.'

'Yes, I believe we have met,' Bart replied, after a thoughtful moment.

While they ate their lunch, Kelsey regaled Bart with some of the adventures of Donald McMurphy that she had not as yet used in her novels.

'Your stepfather sounds like quite a man,' Bart commented. 'I'd like to get to know him better.'

'Maybe we could have a family get-together some

time,' Kelsey suggested. 'I know that Donald was at your parents' wedding, but I don't think my mother has met your mother.' She told Bart what Donald had told her about his long friendship with the Malones.

'Well, I'll be darned,' Bart said. 'Small world, isn't it?' He smiled warmly at Kelsey. 'You know, Miss Cameron, you're the most fascinating woman I've met in a long time.'

'I am?' Kelsey paused with her wine-glass half-way to her mouth and stared at Bart Malone. 'I mean, thank you,' she said, feeling her cheeks grow warm both at the compliment and her inept response. 'But I should think that you'd meet all kinds of fascinating women in your social circles.'

Bart shook his head. 'Not really. A lot that think they are, but have nothing interesting to say. They usually seem to have only one thing on their minds.' He gave a slightly embarrassed laugh. 'What I mean is, the available women my age are still available for a good reason, but they don't know it, and the younger ones just aren't on the same wavelength as I am. It's impossible to establish a friendship when you have the feeling that every move someone makes is calculated to impress you with what a good marriage prospect they are. It makes you feel like a bear with a steel trap in front of him and a pit behind him. I may be overly suspicious, but it's inhibited me from enjoying female company so much that I don't go out much any more, except to concerts and other unromantic events.'

Kelsey took a large swallow of her wine and stared at Bart intently. He was certainly making no bones about the fact that he did not want to be considered a marriage prospect! She had better tell him of her little ploy with Morris Carter before Henry took it upon himself to do so, or he might change his favourable opinion of her in a hurry! She set her wine-glass down and clutched at it as it teetered on its base.

'I—I think it's time we discussed your problem,' she said, nervously. 'You'll be surprised to hear what I've already found out. I was barely in the ambulance when I started hearing that I should sue.' She told him what had happened, reciting Morris Carter's approach to her that morning almost word for word. 'He was obviously trying to turn me against you, warning me like that to stay away because you got rough,' she said, eyeing Bart speculatively before she concluded, 'so I gave him a real shock. I told him that I certainly would, unless I decided to marry you instead.'

'You told him *what?*' Bart said, suddenly sitting up straight in his chair. He quickly leaned toward Kelsey again, his eyes searching her face, an expression of disbelief on his own. 'You told him you were going to marry me?' he repeated hoarsely.

'Please don't get the wrong idea!' Kelsey said hurriedly. 'I don't really want to marry you.' She reached to put her hand on Bart's arm, inadvertently knocking over her empty wine-glass. 'Oh, thank goodness it was empty,' she muttered, righting it and wiping beads of nervous perspiration from her upper lip. If only she had a really good explanation for why she had said that!

'What I was going to say,' she went on, feeling more desperate by the minute as Bart continued to stare at her, 'is that I just wanted to shake Mr Carter up a bit by telling him that. Remember Rake Devlin's theory that people who are confused sometimes make fatal mistakes?' She watched Bart anxiously as he nodded dubiously. Then, like the flash that had inspired her original remark to Morris Carter, it came to her. She smiled triumphantly. 'Well, don't you see? Morris Carter will think I know something very important that he doesn't know. Something that could even give me the power to blackmail you into marrying me!'

Bart Malone frowned. 'Well, that might be helpful, I suppose, but I still don't quite understand how.'

'You're just not used to thinking as deviously as a detective,' Kelsey said. 'Morris Carter will be dying to find out what I know that he doesn't know. He may well come around to see me about it, and that could give us the opening we're looking for.' She studied Bart Malone's face. He was now staring into space, looking very thoughtful. Perhaps he was having second thoughts about a Dawn Daley who made such rash statements. 'I'm sorry if I shocked you more than Morris Carter,' she said. 'It was just a story I made up on the spur of the moment. I'm not planning to get married and, from what you said, it sounds as if you definitely don't ever plan to get married. Or have you been married in the past? I guess I really don't know.'

'No, I haven't,' Bart said, suddenly redirecting his attention to Kelsey. He smiled at her, his grey eyes full of silvery sparks of mischief. 'I'm not in shock, Miss Cameron, although, for a moment there, I thought maybe you were proposing to me.'

'Good heavens, no!' Kelsey said, feeling her cheeks grow warm. Oh, dear, that didn't sound very nice. 'I mean, there's nothing wrong with you, Mr Malone, nothing at all, but . . . I haven't known you very long.'

Bart grinned and leaned his chin on his hand.

'And when you've known me longer, I might hope
for a proposal? I'm not nearly as averse to the idea
of marriage as I may have sounded, if the right
person comes along and makes those bells ring that
you always hear about.'

Kelsey's eyes widened. 'You're baiting me, Mr
Malone. I think I'll plead the fifth amendment on
that. Now maybe we should get on with discussing
your case, unless you have something else you'd like
to say about my crazy statement to Morris Carter.'

'Maybe I should warn you about my mother,' Bart
said, the mischief returning to his eyes. 'She's been
trying to push a young socialite named Fiona at me
lately. I've told her no, thanks, but she doesn't give
up easily. Now, if Morris Carter starts nosing around,
and my mother hears about us . . .'

'Oh, dear!' Kelsey said. 'If your mother thought
you were giving into blackmail by a schoolteacher
when you wouldn't marry her socialite candidate,
she'd be even more anxious than Morris Carter to
know what you'd done, wouldn't she?'

'Quite likely,' Bart replied. 'Mother's something of
a snob.'

'Well, I don't want to make life that difficult for
you,' Kelsey said. 'I'll call Mr Carter and make an
appointment to see him, and leave word that I've
decided to sue you after all. That should scotch any
rumours before they get started. Now, did you bring
that address for the man who lost the finger? I think
I'll put on my neck-brace and hobble off to see him.
I want to find out exactly what Morris Carter told
him in order to persuade him to make such a huge
claim.' Kelsey paused and cocked her head to study
Bart, who was staring at her face but did not seem
to be listening to what she said. 'Why do I have the

feeling you haven't heard a word I've said?' she asked.

Bart smiled suddenly. 'I think I heard most of it,' he said, 'but I was thinking about something else at the same time.' He got to his feet and paced back and forth several times, finally stopping in front of Kelsey's sofa and picking up the rabbit. He looked at it for a few moments, then at Kelsey, who was watching him, trying to guess why on earth he was studying a stuffed rabbit with such deadly seriousness.

'Do you like this?' he asked, raising the rabbit in front of him. 'I mean you, personally. Not the Dawn Daley character.'

'Very . . . very much,' Kelsey replied, surprised at the question. 'I ended up sleeping with him last night, and the doctor teased me about it this morning. I think I'll name him Elwood.' She tilted her head and gave Bart a quizzical look. 'You know, I wondered last night whether you'd have bought him for me if you weren't playing Rake Devlin.'

Bart nodded his head. 'Oh, yes. I certainly would have. Elwood,' he repeated. 'Good name.' He looked over at Kelsey and smiled at her, almost shyly. 'I wasn't sure you'd really like it, either. Some people think stuffed animals are only for little children, but I think adults can find something soft and cuddly very comforting when they're alone in a strange place. A nice dog who can wag his tail is even better, but hospitals don't cope with dogs very well. I tried to smuggle one in to a . . . er . . . young lady I knew once, a long time ago. It caused quite a ruckus.'

Kelsey laughed, finding it suddenly very easy to imagine Bart with a dog hidden beneath his overcoat, smiling nervously and commenting on the weather as he passed the nurses' station. 'That's wonderful,' she said. 'If you're ever in the hospital, do let me know. I'll smuggle in a puppy in a basket, just like Little Red Riding Hood, bringing goodies to her grandma.'

'I'll bet you would, at that,' Bart said. He put the rabbit down, came back to the table, and whirled his chair around so that he could sit on it backwards, with his elbow leaning on the back, his chin on his hand. He looked at Kelsey intently, as if he were trying to work out some difficult problem and her face would give him the answer. She was about to ask him what he was thinking about that was so serious, when he asked bluntly, 'Why don't you want to marry?'

Startled, Kelsey felt as if her brain had evaporated, leaving an empty space in which Bart's words echoed round and round. Marriage, and her attitude towards it, was something she tried to spend as little time as possible thinking about. She had no idea why Bart suddenly wanted to know, but she felt that she should give him a sensible-sounding answer. At last she gathered her wits enough to reply haltingly, 'It's . . . it's not that I'm against marriage, I just don't think I need it. I was engaged once, when I was a senior in college. And then . . . just about seven years ago . . . the young man—his name was Tom—was killed in a road accident. It was a foggy night and the young woman driving the other car was drunk.' She paused, tears filling her eyes. 'She was killed, too, but that doesn't help.'

Bart reached out and touched her hand, his expression so sympathetic that Kelsey was almost undone completely. 'I'm sure it doesn't,' he said softly. 'You needn't say any more.'

Kelsey shook her head and blinked back her tears.

'I try not to think about it,' she said, 'but maybe I should talk about it so I'll get over it.' She looked questioningly at Bart.

'It might help,' he said. 'Go ahead.'

'Well,' Kelsey went on, 'After Tom was killed, for a long time it was as if I couldn't feel anything. Once I got over that, I decided that I didn't want to risk going through it again any time soon. Then, when I got started teaching, I had so many things to do, so many children to care about and help for so many hours a week, that I felt even less inclined to get romantically involved again.' She managed a little smile. 'My parents are always trying to marry me off, too, but I tell them that I'm just too busy.'

Bart nodded, his eyes narrowed and his expression withdrawn. 'Too busy,' he repeated slowly. 'Sometimes I think that's more crippling than any disease.' His voice trailed off, then suddenly he was looking directly at Kelsey, his attention intense and forceful. 'You know, the more I think about it, the more I think you had a brilliant idea, telling Morris Carter that you might marry me. I'm sure he'll come to the conclusion that it's blackmail, and when he does he'll come around, trying to find out what it is that you know. If there's collusion between him and the insurance claims adjuster, as Joe Rocco suggested there might be, that might really drive a wedge between them.'

'That's right!' Kelsey agreed enthusiastically, glad to find that Bart was now on her wavelength. 'Greedy little Morris Carter may well think that he could get a lot more out of you than he ever will from those relatively small claims the insurance company has been paying. He might even offer me a share in order to find out what it is. Then we'd really have him where we want him! I knew there was a good reason why that idea popped into my head the way it did. I mean,' she explained hurriedly, as Bart looked at her curiously, 'that, at the moment I said it, I intuitively knew that it was the right thing to say, but I wasn't really thinking in terms of blackmail. I—I've sometimes helped Mr Rocco with ideas that come to me like that.'

Kelsey felt a rush of relief as Bart's eyes began to twinkle with that spark of mischief that she had noticed several times before. She had gotten herself out of that one, but she had better be careful. She had almost slipped up and said something about how ideas came to her like that when she was writing!

'You may need all the intuition you can muster when my mother gets wind of this,' Bart said with a chuckle. 'When she hears that I'm thinking of marrying you, especially if there's some hint of scandal involved, she'll not only come after me, but you're apt to be descended upon by her in full battle regalia. But if you're still willing to go ahead with it, knowing that, I'm game. I'll find some way to fend her off.'

'Oh, I think I can handle it,' Kelsey said confidently, although mentally she was imagining a buxom woman, costumed like a Teutonic goddess, charging up the hill towards her apartment, sword in hand. 'After all, it will only be for a short while. If the pretence works, we may find out everything you wanted to know in a few days. Then you can go back to just fighting off Fiona.'

'That's not much of an alternative,' Bart said with a wry smile. 'I think our pretence sounds much more interesting.'

'You do?' Kelsey said, startled. She was beginning

to find the whole scenario rather intimidating. It was definitely a lot more nerve-racking than simply writing about it. 'It *is* just a pretence,' she reminded Bart, 'and Morris Carter may not pursue it at all. That's possible, you know.'

Bart nodded. 'I know, but it's worth a try.' He looked at his watch and then stood up. 'I'm afraid I've got several more stops to make this afternoon. Some of my store managers are getting pretty jittery, and it helps if I take the time to talk to them every few days. I'll check back with you later this evening.' He pulled a folded paper from his pocket and handed it to Kelsey. 'This is a list of the plaintiffs from the past year, and a description of their accidents, and a separate sheet I just got on Mr Santos. Do you still plan to visit him today?'

'I think I will,' Kelsey replied. 'I'd like to meet this person whose entire life has been ruined by losing a finger and see what he's really like, and find out a bit about his past. We need to see if we can connect the people who are suing you in any way.'

'Good thinking,' Bart agreed.

Kelsey stood up and held out her hand. 'Well, Mr Malone, our investigation is about to get officially under way. Let's hope the unofficial Malone and Cameron detective agency is up to the job.'

Bart's mouth quirked at the corners in a little smile. 'It will be interesting, no matter what happens, Miss Cameron,' he said, taking her hand. 'But don't you think, if we're supposed to be considering marriage, even a sort of shotgun wedding, that we should be on a first-name basis?'

'I guess we should,' Kelsey agreed, 'Bart.'

'Kelsey.' Bart looked down at Kelsey's hand, which had all but disappeared inside his, then into her eyes, that imp of mischief returning. 'Fiona does have one advantage going for her,' he said. 'She's over six feet tall, which means that she's tall enough that if I did want to kiss her, which I definitely don't, I wouldn't have to break my neck.'

Kelsey laughed. 'Maybe that's the subconscious reason you've never married. Fear of neck trouble. I'm almost five foot eight, but I can see it would still present a problem for you. Did you ever think of carrying a footstool around with you for your lady friends to stand on?'

'That's a good idea,' Bart agreed with a grin. His eyes lifted from Kelsey's to sweep round the room. Without warning, he slid his hands beneath Kelsey's arms and lifted her into the air.

'Mr Malone . . . Bart, put me down. What on earth . . .?' Kelsey stopped, finding herself deposited on the hassock in front of her big armchair, her eyes now almost on a level with Bart's. 'I didn't mean . . . We aren't really . . .' she began, but stopped again, suddenly aware that Bart Malone was going to kiss her, suddenly aware that she was now enveloped in his arms and that she had the dreamy sensation that she was fading into a grey, soft mist that swirled round and round, drawing her ever closer until at last their lips touched. Touched very briefly, then touched and held and pressed together.

At first they were both very still, as if the initial contact had frozen them in place, unable to move. Kelsey had a strange impression of time standing still for the two of them while, all around, the world kept going about its business. It was an exciting feeling, almost electric, and at the same time languorous and lovely. She felt her lips part of their own volition in response to a touch from the tip of Bart's tongue. Her arms found their way round him, to cling to the hard strength beneath the softness of his sweater. While her own tongue played with his in a mad, lovely dance, she felt them tighten their arms about each other, and sensed a warmth building between them. It was a warmth that could become a dangerous heat, where skin caught fire at another's touch and sensible thoughts flew away like wisps of smoke.

While Kelsey's mind registered vaguely that she should end this kiss before that happened, every inch of her body resisted, seeming to enjoy with wanton independence the way that Bart's hands had moved slowly down to her bottom and were tucking her ever more tightly against him. When he made a deep sound of pleasure, she found herself wondering if Bart was planning to act out one of the more torrid scenes she had written between Rake Devlin and Dawn Daley. If so, the next thing he would do was . . .

Oh, no, he won't! Kelsey thought, suddenly touching base with reality. That was definitely not the kind of relationship she planned between Kelsey Cameron and Bart Malone! She put her hand between them and gave Bart a firm but gentle push. A moment later, he loosened his grasp and raised his head.

For a long time, Bart stared at Kelsey, his expression stunned. Then, very carefully, he lifted her down to the floor and released her. Kelsey thought briefly of admonishing him for getting so carried away, but she could see that he was already deeply disturbed by what had happened. Besides, she had to admit to herself that she had, until the very last, been as guilty as he was. She waited, and watched a play of emotions on his face that ranged from serious and thoughtful to wryly amused. All the time he continued to look at her, his head bent forward, his fingers rubbing the side of his neck as he did so. 'I guess I'm not quite sure what to say right now,' he said at last.

Kelsey shook her head. 'Neither am I. Except I wondered why you did that. I was beginning to think that perhaps you were really a little bit shy with women, but that's obviously not the case. Are you sure you aren't going to turn into a regular Rake Devlin?'

Bart smiled crookedly and shook his head. 'I may not be shy, but I'm not quite that dashing. I guess you might say that I had an impulse to kiss you, which is not something that's happened to me often in recent years. Anyway, once we started, it definitely seemed like the right thing to do. I hope you're not offended.'

'Not really,' Kelsey said, thinking that it should have been obvious to Bart during the kiss that she was anything but offended. 'I do impulsive things myself quite often. It was an impulse that made me tell Morris Carter that I might marry you. Sometimes things happen that way. And then it turns out to be a good thing that they did. Of course, you don't always know right away whether it was or not, so you don't know whether to be glad or sorry.'

Bart picked up Kelsey's hand, and studied it intently. 'Right now, I'm glad,' he said at last, letting go of her hand and raising his eyes to Kelsey's, 'and I think I'll stay that way.' He suddenly smiled at her, the broadest smile Kelsey had yet seen him smile, one that set deep lights dancing in the translucent grey of his eyes.

If a fire could be silver, it would look like that,

Kelsey thought, entranced. It made her feel breathless and warm and her voice did not sound as firm as normal when she said, 'It was nice, but I don't think we should make a habit of it. After all, we don't really plan to marry, and you're not Rake Devlin and I'm not Dawn Daley.'

'You're absolutely right,' Bart said, but his smile only faded a little, and Kelsey had the uncomfortable feeling that his agreement had more form than substance to it. Bart Malone was going to need close watching, especially if he got caught up in the role of Rake Devlin. He was apparently a lot less immune to feminine charms than he claimed, even when he was himself!

She was sure of it when he reached out and ruffled her hair familiarly, and then lifted her chin with his finger. 'I want you to be very careful when you go to see Santos,' he said, 'He doesn't live in one of the better parts of town.'

'I can take care of myself,' Kelsey replied tightly, the touch of Bart's hand having started a new series of wavelets of warmth tingling downward in delicious little surges. She backed quickly away. 'Now, if you don't mind, I think I'd better be going. I don't want to get caught in the rush-hour traffic. I'll let you know tonight what happens.' She went to the door and held it open for Bart.

Bart ducked under the door-frame and paused to look down at Kelsey. 'I'll stop by,' he said, then turned and walked briskly to his car.

CHAPTER THREE

KELSEY closed the door behind Bart, then whirled around and walked, just as briskly as he had, in the opposite direction. In an unbroken chain of movements, she scooped up the lists of plaintiffs from her table, picked up her suede jacket and handbag from a kitchen chair, and went out through her back door, closing it firmly behind her. Her mind felt as if it were seething with unformed thoughts, mixed with a *mélange* of memories and dreams that were both real and unreal. She did not want to stop to examine just how they might be related to Bart Malone and his kiss. At the moment, all that she wanted to do was to move, preferably very fast, and try to clear away the cobwebs.

She wriggled into her jacket as she crossed the little bricked patio with its surrounding beds of riotously beautiful begonias, and walls draped with bougainvillaea vines. At the small door into her garage, which always stuck when the weather was damp, she paused and shoved it open with her hip. Then she dug her car keys from the bottom of her bag, settled into the seat of her little Porsche, and pressed the control which raised the garage door. The car started with a comfortingly powerful roar, and Kelsey backed out into the alleyway, closed the garage, and started down the drive with a small screech of her tyres. She took a deep breath and let it out in a long sigh of relief. Maybe now she could get down to the business for which Bart Malone had originally contacted her. The last twenty or so hours had definitely not been what she had originally had in mind!

Kelsey dodged swiftly through the maze of short, steep blocks and narrow, one-way streets of the little town of Manhattan Beach, which perched like a colourful Mediterranean village on its hillside above the blue Pacific Ocean, until she came to a main boulevard which led to one of the freeways that connected the sprawling parts of Los Angeles and its suburbs to each other and the ocean. She was stopped at a traffic light, looking straight ahead, when a honking horn and movement in the periphery of her vision made her aware that the driver in the large car to her right was trying to get her attention.

Just what I need, she thought in disgust. Some idiot who wants to race because I'm driving a Porsche. He would soon learn that that was a foolish idea. She ignored the person's signals and pressed the accelerator heavily when the traffic light turned green. With a screech of tyres, the car to her right roared ahead of her, then cut in close in front, forcing Kelsey to jam on her brakes to keep from hitting it.

Kelsey shook her fist in the window. 'You numbskull!' she yelled, although she knew the driver could not hear her. A large hand and arm stuck out from the driver's window and waved frantically up and down. Kelsey frowned. What was that lunatic in the black Mercedes . . .

'Good lord! It's Bart!' she said aloud. She waved back in recognition, and then saw that Bart was motioning for her to follow him. Now what? she wondered, and followed as he got into the right-hand lane and then turned off on to a side-street, parking next to a service station. Kelsey parked behind him and got out of her car at the same time as Bart emerged from his and came towards her.

'What on earth possessed you . . .?' she began, but stopped as soon as she saw what Bart held in his hand. It was her neck-brace. 'Oh, dear,' she said, feeling incredibly stupid as she took it from him and fastened it round her neck. Some detective she was turning out to be! Bart was well ahead of her. 'How did you happen to discover that I forgot this?' she demanded. 'How did you get into my apartment? And why?'

Bart gave her a bemused smile. 'I didn't realise that you wanted to race back there. As to how I discovered you'd forgotten your neck-brace, I decided that I didn't think you should go to see Santos alone, after all. When you didn't answer your door, I opened it. I've still got your key from feeding your cat. I saw the neck-brace lying on the table. When I discovered you'd already left, I thought I'd better try to catch up with you. Does that answer all of your questions?'

'I guess so,' Kelsey replied, giving Bart a sideways glance, 'but you're not coming with me. I don't know how you imagine I could find out anything at all with you along.'

'I didn't plan on going to the house,' Bart said. 'I thought I'd just park nearby where I could keep an eye on things.'

'Oh, for heaven's sake!' Kelsey snorted. 'In that?' She pointed at Bart's Mercedes. 'You'd be as conspicuous as a fire engine! You might as well come riding into that neighbourhood on an elephant!'

'Yours isn't exactly what everyone thereabouts will be driving, either,' Bart said drily. 'Or hadn't that occurred to you?'

'It had, but I'm not necessarily trying to be inconspicuous,' Kelsey replied defensively. 'Besides, my car is twelve years old and it looks it. Yours is almost new. Now, just go on about your business and stop trying to play Rake Devlin.'

'I suppose a new Mercedes isn't the right car for surveillance, is it?' Bart said, ignoring Kelsey's orders and frowning thoughtfully. 'What kind of car is it that Rake Devlin uses? A seventy-nine Chevy?'

'Bart, will you listen to me?' Kelsey said, her voice rising impatiently. 'I do not want you following me around. I do not *need* you to follow me.'

'You forgot your neck-brace,' Bart pointed out calmly. 'You needed that.' He looked toward the service station. 'Say, look at that,' he said, smiling. 'That might be just what I need. I wonder how much they want for it? Come on, let's ask.'

Kelsey turned around and immediately saw what Bart saw. Parked in the corner of the service station forecourt was an old blue Plymouth sedan with a 'For Sale' sign in the front window. 'I don't have time . . .' she began, but Bart had taken a firm grip on her arm, and she was in danger of being pulled through the air like a kite if she did not go along with him. 'Quit it!' she said, trying to wrench her arm free. 'People will think I'm wearing this neck-brace because you abused me.'

Bart dropped her arm and gave Kelsey a severe look. 'You know I would never do that,' he said.

'How do I know?' she retorted. 'I've known you for less than a day.' She suddenly found herself face to face with Bart, who stopped dead in front of her, took her shoulders in his hands, and bent to peer into her face.

'I'd rather die than harm you or let any harm come to you,' he said seriously, a frown making a vertical crease between his brows. 'I hope you believe me.'

'I . . . I do,' Kelsey replied, hot tears suddenly coming to her eyes. 'I don't know why I said that. I'm sorry.' Nor was she sure why she felt like crying, except that she could tell that she had hurt Bart's feelings with her thoughtless remark, and it made her feel terrible. Now, she could see that the sight of a tear trickling down her cheek had made him feel uncomfortable, which didn't help, either. She sniffed and looked past his shoulder. A man in overalls, wiping his greasy hands on an equally greasy rag, was coming towards them. 'I think the service station man's coming over here to see what we're doing,' she said, hoping to distract Bart from their impasse. 'He probably knows about the car.'

Bart nodded but was not distracted. He pulled a handkerchief from his pocket and dabbed carefully at Kelsey's tears. 'Are you all right?' he asked, taking her chin between his fingers and studying her face intently.

'I'm fine. Really,' she replied, knowing that she lied. She had not been fine since she slipped and the banana tree attacked her. She had seen stars, then, and Prince Charming, and today a grey fog that swirled around and carried her away. Maybe she *had* knocked something loose when her head hit the floor. Maybe she would have to sue Bart Malone. Or marry him! Kelsey looked at Bart and tried to feel like laughing at such a ridiculous thought, but somehow she did not find it even slightly amusing. Instead, there was a funny feeling in the pit of her stomach and she could feel her heart thumping irregularly.

While Bart talked to the man and examined the car, Kelsey stood nearby and watched and nodded helpfully when Bart looked at her, but scarcely heard a word that they said. She found herself studying Bart from head to foot, noticing the way he gestured with his large, slender hands, looking at the way his dark hair grew thick and neat, trimmed just above the collar of the white silk shirt that he wore beneath his grey sweater. He could be described as an angular man, she decided, the way his shoulders were wide and square to his neck, and his hip jutted out when he shifted his weight from one foot to the other. But his face was a combination of angles and curves, an oval shape with brows that swept outwards above a rather long nose that was as straight as an arrow and a mouth that curved easily into a smile. He was handsome, but there was not a trace of arrogance about him, in spite of his athletic skills and his wealth. He had an easy self-assurance that commanded respect without intimidation. She could see that the service station man and Bart were having a mutually friendly interchange. Now Bart was smiling warmly and shaking the man's hand. Oh, no! Had he decided to buy that old car?

'I think that's a good idea, don't you?' Bart said, turning towards Kelsey.

'Terrific!' she replied, not wanting to admit that she had no idea what he was talking about.

'Good. Then I'll park the Mercedes here while we go to the Santoses', and have Henry pick it up later. Then I'll gas up the old Plymouth, and you can follow me on to the Santoses' street. That way, if anything should go wrong with the car, you'll be there to rescue me.' Bart grinned at Kelsey's blank stare, then strode off to get his Mercedes.

'You won't have no trouble with this old baby,' the service station man said positively, patting the old car, 'and it'll make a good extra car for you folks.'

'I'm sure it will,' Kelsey said numbly. Bart, apparently, had indeed decided to buy the car, determined that he was going to keep watch while she visited the Santos family. With a resigned sigh, she went back to her little Porsche and quickly got herself in position to follow Bart when he was ready. It would be quite easy to lose him if she wanted to take off in her fast and manoeuvrable sports car, but he would just turn up at the Santoses' address anyway, probably both angry and hurt that she was trying to avoid him. Oh, well. It was very sweet of him to be so concerned. Sweet, but totally unnecessary.

The old car proved to be far speedier than Kelsey would have believed possible, leading them to their destination almost as swiftly as she would have expected to get there alone. She parked her car a couple of houses down from the Santoses' address and got out, noticing that Bart, who had gone on around the block, now slowly came back and stopped across the street, in a location that gave him a good view and quick access to both the Santoses' house and her car if he was needed. Obviously, she thought to herself with a smile, he had paid close attention to Rake Devlin's technique.

Cars filled with teenagers were cruising up and down the street, and there were loud sounds of rock-and-roll music blaring from both the cars and the windows of several of the houses. It was, Kelsey knew, a neighbourhood where there had been some trouble with teenage gangs, but recently a shaky truce had been declared. At the moment, all the noise seemed good-humoured. There were children's toys littered around the small garden of the Santoses' little house, indicating to Kelsey's quick eye that several children, from kindergarten age to perhaps ten or eleven, lived there. A small girl of about six came to the door when Kelsey knocked and stood staring at her, wide-eyed and silent.

'Is your daddy Robert Santos?' Kelsey asked.

The little girl nodded.

'I came to see your daddy. I heard that he got hurt at a store, and I did too,' Kelsey said, pointing to her neck-brace. 'I wanted to ask him some questions, if he wouldn't mind.'

The door closed again, and Kelsey heard the child shouting to her father and mother that there was a lady there to see her daddy. Soon the door opened again, and a harried-looking woman, with a baby in her arms and another toddler clinging to her legs, stood there. 'What d'you want?' she asked coldly.

Kelsey fidgeted and pulled on her neck-brace as if it hurt her to move. 'My name's Cameron. I got hurt over at the Big Winner store, and I heard that your husband did too,' she said. 'A lawyer named Carter came to see me, but I don't know whether to trust him or not. I was wondering if I could talk to Mr Santos for a minute.'

The woman shrugged. 'Sure. Why not?' She stood aside for Kelsey to enter. 'Just sit down there,' she said, pointing to a dilapidated chair. 'I'll get him.'

Kelsey sat, her eyes quickly sweeping around the clutter of the small living-room of a house that was obviously strained past capacity by the large family it housed. It was, she thought sadly, a not unfamiliar sight to someone who had taught in some of the less privileged neighbourhoods. In a few moments, a sad-eyed young man entered, clutching one hand, which was swathed in bandages, with the other.

'Sorry I can't shake hands,' he said by way of introduction, 'but it still throbs like the devil.'

'I'm so sorry about your accident,' Kelsey said, feeling a real twinge of sympathy for him. 'I'm not so good at hopping up and down myself, right now. But I guess I'm lucky it wasn't a lot worse.'

Exploiting the fact that misery loved company, Kelsey soon had Robert Santos conversing about their mutual disasters as if they were old friends. Once she had described her accident, he was perfectly willing to tell her about his.

'This guy in front of me put a twenty-dollar bill down on the conveyor belt,' he said. 'When I saw it was going to go down into the crack, I made a grab for it. He must have thought I was going to steal it. He pounded down on my hand with his fist like he was trying to break a rock. That forced my little finger into the crack. Then, when I tried to jerk it back out . . .'

'How awful,' Kelsey said, grimacing as she imagined the gory scene. 'What did the man say when he saw what he'd done?'

'As soon as he saw, he ran like a deer,' Robert Santos said disgustedly. 'And the dumb clerk fainted. It took me almost five minutes to get someone to call an ambulance. I'd about decided to drive myself, even with the blood dripping all over, when they showed up.'

Kelsey clucked sympathetically. Mr Santos, she thought, either had a very great talent for acting or he was a genuine victim. Perhaps not to the extent he claimed, but he definitely did not look as though he was faking it.

'You certainly have a legitimate cause for complaint,' she said, 'but it's a lot worse problem than mine. At least, the way it seems right now. I don't know exactly what to do.'

'Sue them,' Robert Santos said firmly. 'And don't be bashful about asking for plenty. You've got one of those back injuries that might never get better, and could get a lot worse. Besides, there's not much chance you'll get turned down if you've got old Morris Carter on your side. I don't know what his angle is, but he never seems to lose against the Malones.'

'You think he has some kind of angle?' Kelsey asked, giving Robert Santos a wide-eyed look. 'What do you mean?'

Robert Santos smiled and shrugged. 'Who knows? I don't ask. I'm just glad he does. Now I can move my family to a better neighbourhood.'

'Oh? You're that sure of the outcome?' Kelsey looked questioning, hoping for more, but all that Robert Santos did was nod. She frowned and pretended to be in a quandary. 'It would be nice to be able to pay my bills for a change,' she said. 'A schoolteacher's salary doesn't go very far these days.'

'I'll bet it doesn't,' Robert Santos said sympathetically. 'You ladies work awfully long hours for the little bit you get, too. You take my advice and sue that Big Winner outfit. You'll be able to take some really nice vacations.'

'I'll certainly think about it seriously, Mr Santos,' Kelsey said, getting to her feet as if her back was very painful. She walked to the door, accompanied by Robert Santos. 'Thank you very much for talking to me. I certainly hope you feel better soon.'

'I hope you do, too,' he replied.

Kelsey nodded. 'Thank you. I think I'll feel a lot better as soon as I decide whether to sue Bart Malone or persuade him he ought to marry me.' She smiled into the dumbfounded stare of Robert Santos. 'Do take care,' she said, and went out of the door.

She hurried to her car without a backward glance, noticing out of the corner of her eye that Bart's car appeared empty. Apparently he had had the presence of mind to duck out of sight, just as his hero Rake Devlin would have done. She hoped he would stay there until well after Robert Santos had closed his door. That young man, she was sure, was not anyone's fool, and might well peer out of a window to see if there was someone with her.

Kelsey had just unlocked the door to her car when a long, low convertible full of teenage boys pulled up alongside, whistling and making lewd remarks. She ignored them, but before she could slip inside her car, several of the youths had piled out of their car, their approach reminding Kelsey of a film she had recently seen of hyenas about to attack a fallen wildebeest. She managed to throw her handbag into her car, but one of them grabbed her arm and pulled her back before she could follow.

'Aw, looky,' he said, taking hold of Kelsey's neck-brace, 'her boyfriend must've got a little rough with her.' He leered unpleasantly into Kelsey's face. Kelsey took a deep breath, about to begin kicking and screaming for all she was worth. 'You ain't seen nothin' yet, sweetie,' he went on. 'I'm gonna show you . . .'

Kelsey never found out what the young man had in mind, for his mouth suddenly opened wide, his eyes bulged, and he let out a little croaking sound. Bart had picked him up and thrown him with a loud thump across the hood of the convertible, as if he were no heavier than a beachball.

'Get the hell out of here, all of you!' Bart growled, turning round and impaling each of the remaining boys with a challenging stare, 'and don't any of you ever bother a lady again!' The boys took one look at Bart's broad shoulders and towering height. Without saying a single word and with only a few feeble, defiant gestures, the group dissolved back into their car and then sped away.

Bart put his arm around Kelsey's shoulders and leaned forward to look at her anxiously. 'Are you all right?' he asked.

'I—I'm not sure,' she replied, still feeling shaken. 'That was . . . impressive. But you may have blown your cover, leaping out of your car like that and playing Rake Devlin.'

'Playing Rake Devlin?' Bart frowned down at Kelsey. 'For heaven's sake, what did you think I was here for? To hide in that car and pretend I was playing detective while those juvenile delinquents mauled you?'

'Well . . . no,' Kelsey replied slowly. 'I guess not. But I didn't really expect . . .' She stopped. When she wrote about Rake Devlin's exploits, she had always assumed that he was better than any real man would be. But Bart had been every bit as good, almost as if it were second nature to him. He didn't have to pretend at all! Kelsey smiled weakly. 'Thank goodness you were here,' she said.

Bart nodded in agreement. 'Let's get out of here,' he said. 'Those kids may have gone for reinforcements. Turn around and follow me.'

Before Kelsey could say anything more, he ran back across the street and got into his car. She did as he had told her, the sense of something like *déjà vu* that she had felt earlier returning. This time a single thought intruded. Tom. Bart was so much like him. The thought made Kelsey bite her lip and clutch her steering-wheel more tightly. No, he wasn't. No one was like Tom, nor ever would be. Besides, she hardly knew Bart. One stuffed rabbit and a daring rescue did *not* a total person make.

'You looked like Superman, flying across that street this afternoon,' she remarked, when they were back at her apartment. 'I didn't know you knew self-defence.'

Bart gave Kelsey a strange look. 'I don't,' he said, 'but when I saw those kids coming after you . . . I think I could have picked up one in each hand and thrown them about a mile. I don't think I ever felt quite that angry before.' He stared pensively at a piece of the pizza that Kelsey had bought to prevent him from sending for any more of Pierre's elaborate meals. 'If you go to see any more of the plaintiffs that live in dubious neighbourhoods,' he said at last, 'we'd better both go in that old Plymouth. That car of yours is just like bait for a gang of teenagers.'

'I think you're right,' Kelsey agreed, 'but I don't plan to do that for a while. I expect the next person I should see is Morris Carter, but I won't be able to do that until Monday. I wonder what Robert Santos thought if he saw you.'

'Did you tell him that you were thinking of marrying me?'

Kelsey nodded. 'It seemed to astound him completely, too.' She smiled wryly. 'The funny part of it is, I never suggested to either him or Morris Carter that there was any blackmail involved, but they both responded as if that was the first thought that came to their minds. I guess I don't look like your type.'

Bart smiled, an imp of mischief briefly lighting his eyes. 'Maybe if he saw me he thought that I'm following you around. That it's one of those unrequited love cases, and I'm a pest you can't get rid of. That would add an interesting complication.'

'Too interesting,' Kelsey replied. 'Things are complicated enough already. I'm going to need crib-notes to keep them straight. I don't think I have much natural talent for this line of work. It's a lot easier to sit and figure it out on paper like I used to do for Joe Rocco.'

'Most things are,' Bart commented drily. He lapsed into a brooding silence and was quiet for so long that Kelsey began to wonder if he felt ill.

'Do you feel all right?' she asked at last.

Bart looked at her curiously, his eyes strangely intent. 'Why do you ask that?'

'Because you're so quiet,' Kelsey replied. 'I thought maybe you strained your back, throwing that boy around like you did.'

'My back's fine,' Bart replied, shaking his head, but he still appeared distracted, although he was looking directly at Kelsey.

'Don't you want to hear what Mr Santos told me?' she asked.

'Of course,' he said. 'What . . . what did he have to say?'

'Nothing specific. I think he's too smart for that. But he did say that he was sure Morris Carter had what he called an angle that made it possible for him to succeed in suits against your stores, and he's very sure of the outcome of his own suit. He's already planning to move his family to a better neighbourhood. He strongly advised me to sue. I can't think of any angle he could have, except an arrangement with the claims adjuster, can you?'

Bart stared into space for so long before he answered that Kelsey wondered if he had heard her. But finally he did say quietly, 'No, I can't say that I can.'

His behaviour, Kelsey thought, was very strange. It was almost as if he were lost deeply in thought on some entirely different subject. Well, perhaps he was worried about something that had happened at one of his stores today. After all, he had many responsibilities to cope with besides the lawsuits. It might be a good idea if she did as much as possible on her own.

'I think I'll call Donald in the morning and see if he can find out for us if this fellow Edgerton, the claims adjuster, is a solid citizen. I'm sure Donald still has contacts who could do that.'

Bart looked at Kelsey strangely for a moment, then nodded. 'Good idea,' he agreed without enthusiasm.

In an effort to get his mind on something more cheerful, Kelsey changed the subject. 'Does your family have a big get-together for Easter?' she asked. 'My sister and her husband and their three children and I always go to visit my mother and stepfather. They have a little ranch near Santa Barbara where they keep ponies for the children to ride, and some ducks and chickens. We colour Easter eggs the night before and then hide the eggs outside for the kids to hunt for in the morning, until it's time to get dressed up for church. I'll take Elwood along this year. He'll be a bit hit.'

'That sounds nice and traditional,' Bart said with a grimace so sour that Kelsey wished she hadn't brought up the subject. 'We'll have the usual gathering of the clan at my uncle's place in Laguna Beach. Uncle Dan and my father will argue about business and politics, my mother and my aunt will tear each other's friends and acquaintances apart, and my dozens of cousins will fight over whatever is appropriate to their age group. My brother, if he shows up, will get drunk and try to seduce any female who isn't too young or too closely related. That's the standard Malone holiday celebration.'

Kelsey wanted to use the opportunity to find out more about Bart's brother, whom Donald had described as the black sheep, but the chaotic image that his description produced was too much for her. She knew he meant it seriously, but in her mind's eye she saw a Marx Brothers' free-for-all, with the adults throwing pies at each other, the children riding ponies through the dining-room, and Bart's brother chasing nubile females from room to room and peering down their bosoms. She bit her lip, choked, then started to giggle. Bart shot her a dark look, which only made it worse. Her giggles turned to howls of helpless laughter, until tears were running down her cheeks.

'I'm s-sorry,' she gasped, 'but it sounded so . . . so crazy!' She tried to stop, but the sight of Bart staring at her as if she were crazy, too, sent her into fresh peals of laughter. Then, suddenly, Bart grinned, chuckled a little and finally ended up roaring with laughter as uncontrollable as Kelsey's.

'Thank heaven for someone with perspective,' he said, when he had finally stopped and begun mopping his eyes. 'I don't think I'll ever be able to take it all as seriously again.'

Kelsey smiled, delighted that she had lifted Bart

out of his gloomy mood. 'I hope it doesn't get you into trouble. You know, you hadn't even mentioned that you had a brother. Do you have any other siblings?'

Bart shook his head. 'No, just the one. I didn't know you had a sister, either. What is she like? Is she a teacher too?'

Was Bart being polite, or was he avoiding discussing his brother? Kelsey wondered before she answered. 'My sister's not much like me. She never wanted a career. She loves being a homemaker, and she thinks I'm crazy for not wanting to get married. I don't find fault with her for living the way she does, so we have arguments sometimes when I won't go out with some friend of hers and her husband's. What's your brother like? Is he as tall as you are?'

'No, he's nothing like me. Ford's just over six feet tall and very handsome,' Bart replied, somewhat defensively, Kelsey thought. 'He's always gotten by on his charm and looks. I guess some people would call him a playboy, but I don't, because that has negative connotations. I envy him his ability to enjoy life without feeling guilty every minute that he isn't working. I've tried to emulate him a few times, usually with disastrous results.' Bart made a wry face. 'I guess I was born with my nose to the grindstone, and I'm doomed to keep it there.'

'It doesn't seem to have shortened it,' Kelsey teased gently, hoping to bring a smile to Bart's again gloomy features.

Instead, Bart shook his head and sighed deeply. 'No, it doesn't, does it?' he said. 'I guess it was made for the job.' He pushed his chair back and got to his feet. 'Kelsey,' he said, 'I'm afraid I'm going to have to call off this whole thing. It's turning out to be more than I can handle right now.' He strode to the door and then stopped, while Kelsey stared at him, open-mouthed. 'It's been very interesting, Kelsey,' he said. 'I'm glad that I met you. Give my regards to Joe Rocco.' Moments later, the door slammed behind him.

CHAPTER FOUR

STUNNED, Kelsey stared after Bart, tears welling in her eyes and a terrible, sick feeling in the pit of her stomach. Was it something she had done? Something she had said? Of course. It must have been that stupid remark she made to Morris Carter. Bart had seemed to adjust to it all right, but perhaps he hadn't been really comfortable with the idea. But then he had kissed her, and for a few moments she had felt more wonderful than she had in a long, long time. Now he had gone, and the world seemed like a cold, empty, dark place, just as it had after Tom . . .

Her tears spilled over in spite of her efforts to fight them back, and she got angrily to her feet. 'What is wrong with you, Kelsey Cameron?' she scolded, picking up the almost untouched pizza and carrying it into her kitchen. 'It's not the same at all! You were in love with Tom.' But the feeling did not go away. She tried to comfort herself with the fact that Bart was not really gone, but it did little good. The more she tried to analyse what had happened, the less she felt she understood why Bart had left. He had seemed quite happy about their adventure until they got back from the Santoses' house. After that, he had got progressively worse, except when she made him laugh over his family's foibles. The mention of his brother had ended that brief reprieve. He had seemed very unhappy about the contrasts between the two of them.

'If only I hadn't said that about his nose,' Kelsey murmured sadly. But that, she knew, was not the real problem. Something had happened that afternoon . . . but what?

While she mechanically went about the business of cleaning up her kitchen and putting things away, Kelsey tried to think objectively, like a detective, about the events that had taken place during the short time since she and Bart had met. There was still no answer to exactly why there had been a rash of lawsuits against the Big Winner stores, but there seemed to be no doubt that there was a concerted and possibly co-operative effort to persuade people to sue them. Could Bart's brother somehow be involved? That didn't seem likely but one did hear of power struggles in families of the wealthy. If Bart had picked up some clue that Ford was mixed up in the suits, that might explain why he had decided to call off their investigation. He seemed unhappy about the negative image that Ford already had. Rather than have something come to light which might send his brother to gaol and cause a great deal of embarrassment and sorrow to him and the rest of the family, he would deal with the problem privately. Still, that didn't seem to be a reason for Bart to say goodbye to her forever. He had said that he was glad that he kissed her. Maybe, when the lawsuit problem was solved, he would come back.

'And maybe he won't,' Kelsey muttered morosely. She went back into her living-room and flopped down on her sofa next to Elwood, who sat propped in one corner with the cat curled up between his stubby legs. Devil yowled a complaint when she picked up the rabbit and hugged him to her, then jumped down from the sofa and stalked away, his tail a perpendicular flag of protest.

'Go ahead, you walk out on me too,' Kelsey said,

burying her cheek in the soft plush of the rabbit. 'I guess no one likes me as much as I thought they did.' That overwrought statement made the ache start in her chest again. To forestall any more tears, she put the rabbit down and got back on her feet. 'Sorry, Elwood,' she said, 'but I'd better get my mind on something else.' Her eye fell on the neat pile of papers which Bart had left on the table, so she picked it up and began scanning through the descriptions of the lawsuits. She could use such things in her writing, if nowhere else.

For a short time, Kelsey paced in circles round her living-room, reading the carefully-worded descriptions of the 'accidents' that had befallen the plaintiffs. Bart had certainly been right that the accidents were bizarre. The first victim had been knocked down by an automatic door, which suddenly opened in his face. He had received a broken nose and a concussion. The second was getting a can of tomatoes off a bottom shelf, when a whole cascade of cans fell on his head from above and rendered him unconscious. The third stopped suddenly to pick up a bag of potatoes and was rammed from behind by another person's shopping trolley with such force that his ribs were broken against the handle of his own trolley. The others were equally strange, and Kelsey could find no logic in the way that it was decided that the Big Winner stores were at fault. Perhaps collusion between the lawyer and the claims adjuster was the answer to that, but how would that involve Ford Malone?

I'd like to talk this all over with Donald tomorrow, Kelsey thought with a sigh. She hated to think that Bart's brother was a criminal, but if Bart did not want to continue trying to solve the case . . . Kelsey bit her lip and shook her head. She would see how she felt tomorrow. Maybe, in the meantime, she would hear from Bart again.

In the morning, Kelsey was up with the birds, feeling as if she had hardly slept at all. Between the intriguing, maddening questions that plagued her about the suspicious lawsuits, and the even more upsetting questions her mind dwelt on after midnight, when she realised that even at that hour she was listening and hoping that Bart would have second thoughts and call her, she had heard almost every 'cuckoo' from her cuckoo-clock.

'I'm afraid you're going to have to wing-it alone until tomorrow,' Kelsey said to Devil, as she filled his little overnight feeder and refilled his water bowl. 'I am not going to hang around here all morning waiting for the telephone to ring.' Fifth-grade teachers did not droop like pallid teenagers. They went on with their lives. If Bart Malone called after she got back from her weekend, fine. If he wanted to leave her alone, that was just fine too.

Kelsey put on a blue velour track-suit, gathered up the bag of Easter eggs and gifts she had purchased for her two nieces and her nephew, and tucked Elwood under her arm. She was almost ready to go out of her back door when there was a knock at the front. Her heart did a little flip-flop and started racing. Could it be Bart? She hurried to the door and peered out through her fish-eye viewing lens. No, it wasn't Bart, but it was a man. He was standing at the edge of her porch, his back to the door. Beyond him in the street was a bright red Maserati. Who could it be? Kelsey wondered. No one she knew drove a car like that. She felt a little chill go through her. Any number of unsavoury people might be interested in the notion that she had some way of persuading Bart to marry her. If Ford Malone was involved and he had heard, he might be very interested! For several minutes Kelsey dithered over whether or not to open her door. The security chain was in place. She wouldn't have to let him in.

While Kelsey watched, the man turned around. There was no doubt about it. From Bart's description, she knew it was his brother. His nose was a little shorter, his face a little broader, and he was very handsome. He also looked very arrogant, walking back to her door and pounding on it with unnecessary force. Kelsey hesitated another moment, then very quietly opened the door a crack.

'Would you mind not beating my door down?' she said coolly. 'Who are you, and what do you want?'

'My name is Ford Malone,' was the reply, 'and I'd like to talk to you about my brother.'

Kelsey frowned and opened the door as far as the chain would permit. 'I'm sorry, Mr Malone, but I am about to leave for the weekend. And I don't want to talk to you. I'd suggest that you talk to your brother yourself. I don't think you two are communicating very well.'

Ford Malone leaned forward, an unpleasantly hostile scowl on his face. For a moment he stared at Kelsey through the opening, then an expression of disbelief took over his face. 'You're Kelsey Cameron?' he said, in almost awestruck tones.

'That's right,' she replied, stepping back a few inches. Ford Malone's sensuality was overwhelming, the gleam in his deep hazel eyes almost tangible. Handsome was an understatement where this man was concerned!

'Well, well,' Ford said, his mouth curving into a smile that made the gleam in his eyes turn into a series of scintillating sparks. 'I had no idea you'd be so gorgeous,' he said in a seductive, soft voice. 'So you're the lovely creature who thinks she's going to marry Bart. Now I really know what we have to talk about. You can do a lot better than holding a gun to the head of that tall stick of a brother of mine, Kelsey. Let me in, so we can discuss your . . . er . . . other options.'

Almost as if some evil witch had waved her magic wand, Kelsey noticed that the moment Ford Malone insulted his brother his appearance suddenly changed from alluringly handsome to disgustingly dissipated and suggestive. She glared at him. 'I have no idea what you're talking about,' she said icily, 'nor do I have any intention of standing here, in my own house, and permitting you to insult me. I am an unmarried schoolteacher by choice. If and when I decide to marry, I will certainly not need to hold a gun to anyone's head. Now, if you will please get your hand out of my door . . .' She nodded towards Ford's fingers, which were holding on to the door-frame.

Ford Malone's expression became angry. 'I don't care if you are a schoolteacher,' he growled. 'You'd better be damned careful you know who you're playing games with.'

'And you'd better get your hand out of my door! Right now!' Kelsey snapped, her own temper flaring. 'I mean it!' Ford's eyes narrowed and his hand did not move. 'Oh, so you don't believe me,' Kelsey said softly. 'Sometimes my students don't, either. The first time. Watch closely what happens on the count of three.' She fixed her eyes on Ford's and counted, 'One, two, three!' then kicked the door shut with all her might, feeling almost weak with relief that he had moved his fingers in time. Otherwise, he might have joined Robert Santos in the missing fingers brigade! Donald

McMurphy had long ago convinced her that she should not shrink from firm action if she felt threatened, but she had really not wanted to find herself in possession of several extra fingers on her side of the door.

Nor did Kelsey want to wait around long enough to find out that Ford Malone was so angry as to try and break into her apartment. She fled out through her back door and got into her car as fast as she could but, when she opened the garage door behind her, Ford Malone was already there in his sports car, blocking her way. 'All right, if that's the way you want it,' she muttered, revving her car's engine. She leaned her head out of her window. 'One, two, three!' she shouted, and threw it into reverse. 'He learns fast,' she said, smiling grimly as Ford shot out of her way in a cloud of dust. She wheeled round and went in the opposite direction, giving a fair imitation of a Grand Prix racer as she headed for the freeway.

All the way to the McMurphys' ranch, Kelsey kept a close watch on her rearview mirror. Although there was no sign of Ford Malone's Maserati, an eerie feeling of unreality pursued her. Warren Wickersham III lived! More and more it seemed as if *The Case of the Crooked Claims* was becoming a real-life drama, with Kelsey Cameron nowhere near as adept as Dawn Daley at dealing with the villains. For, as she thought back over what had happened, she was sure that she had handled Ford Malone's visit very badly. The way he first leered and then glowered at her, she had not felt safe, standing there with only that slim safety-chain between him and the entrance to her apartment. As a result, she had more or less blurted out that she didn't really plan to make Bart marry her. Now, when the fact that he had come seemed to destroy her hopes that Ford had nothing to do with the rash of accidents and lawsuits, she had no way to lure him back if she wanted to. Not that Bart would want her to, anyway. Poor Bart. She knew now that she cared deeply about Bart Malone and hated to see him hurt, especially by a brother who seemed to care far less about Bart than Bart did about him.

It did not take Kelsey's mother and stepfather long to decipher the fact that something was upsetting her, but she refused to answer their queries, except to say that she was stuck in the middle of a mystery.

'Anything I can do to help?' Donald asked.

'It's not that kind of stuck,' Kelsey answered with a sigh.

Her mother eyed Kelsey suspiciously. 'If you weren't almost twenty-nine years old, I'd think you were stuck on a boy . . . or a man, I guess you'd have to call it in your case.'

'That's just because you're dying to get me married off,' Kelsey retorted, at the same time wondering if she was going to be blessed with the same kind of laser-like intuition when she became a mother. She declined her parents' invitation to stay for a few extra days during the Easter vacation and give her brain a rest. 'I'll just end up with a terrible case of writer's block,' she told them, and headed back to Manhattan Beach on Sunday evening, cursing herself for being a silly fool but unable to stay away from her apartment and telephone any longer.

Kelsey had no sooner put her car away in the garage and turned on the outside light than she noticed a sheet of white paper taped to the back door. She hurried across the yard, shifting the burden of Elwood and the large plastic bag of food which her mother had insisted on sending home with her, as she went. She reached for the paper, which was folded in the middle. Opening it, she read the brief message: 'Kelsey—please call me at this number as soon as you get home. Bart.' Below was a telephone number. Her fingers fumbled in her eagerness as she pushed the key into the lock, opened the door, and rushed across her apartment to the telephone in her living-room, dumping her burdens on the sofa as she went.

An unfamiliar male voice answered her call. 'May I speak to Bart Malone, please?' she said.

'Yeah. Just a minute,' was the reply. She heard a voice bellow, 'Bart! It's for you,' and then a few minutes later he answered.

'This is Bart Malone.'

'Hello, Bart, this is Kelsey,' she said breathlessly. 'I got your note.'

'You're home already?' Bart sounded almost startled. Then he gave a short laugh. 'Of course you are, or you wouldn't have gotten my note. Hang on a minute. There's so much noise here I can't hear.' A few moments later he came back on the line. 'May I come over?' he asked. 'I need to talk to you.'

'Of course. I—I'll be right here,' Kelsey replied, feeling weak with relief. Thank goodness Bart had apparently reconsidered his decision to shut her out of his life. But why? 'I guess I'll find out soon enough,' she said to herself with a sigh. She wouldn't mind at all if it was only because he wanted to see her. It would not be much fun to pursue the lawsuit problem and help reveal his brother's involvement in the plot.

To calm herself while she waited, Kelsey carried her packages and Elwood to the kitchen. She put the dinner leftovers into the refrigerator, and set the huge slab of chocolate cake which her mother had sent on her kitchen table. Maybe, she thought, she could get Bart to eat most of that, before she completely destroyed her diet for the next month. It was bad enough to have the cake, but her mother had also sent a small container of fudge icing, in the belief that, as licking the icing bowl had always cheered Kelsey up when she was small, having her own little supply of extra icing might comfort her now. Next, Kelsey sat Elwood down on a kitchen chair and dampened a sponge to try and clean off the sticky spots that hugs from her nieces had left behind. She had only begun when there was a knock on her door.

That was fast, Kelsey thought, wiping her hands on a towel as she went to answer. Almost too fast, considering how far Bart had to come. She peered carefully through her viewing lens, but could see nothing but a dark coat. The knock sounded again.

'Who is it?' she called.

'It's me, Bart,' said a familiar husky voice. 'Who else were you expecting?'

Kelsey's heart skipped, and she threw open the bolt and slid off the security chain. 'Hi!' she said, feeling an almost overwhelming flood of warmth at the sight of the tall man standing there in his dark grey trenchcoat. 'Come on in.'

'Thank you,' Bart said formally, giving her a little smile. 'I'm glad to see you're careful.' He slipped his coat off, then held it over his arm. 'Before I do anything else, I want to apologise for leaving the way I did the other night,' he said seriously. 'It was unforgivable of me, but I hope you'll forgive me anyway.'

'Of course I will,' Kelsey said quickly. 'I was pretty upset, but . . . I thought you must have some reason.'

'I thought I did, too,' Bart said. He smiled suddenly, with a warmth so tangible that Kelsey felt as if the sun had decided to reappear in her apartment. 'But after I'd thought some things through, I decided that I'd made a mistake. Believe me, it won't happen again. Unless, of course, you throw me out.'

'I wouldn't even try that,' Kelsey said, smiling back at him. 'Let me take your coat.' She held out her hand to take it from him. 'This looks like the perfect coat for a detective.' She took it and held the long coat up in front of her. 'I could really hide from the bad guys in this.'

'I can't help being tall,' Bart said gruffly. 'It was great for basketball, but the rest of the time it's a damned nuisance.'

Kelsey looked up at him, her heart suddenly pierced by a terrible ache at the pain she saw in his eyes. Someone, some *idiot*, had made him feel very unhappy about his height. Maybe someone like Ford, who called Bart a 'tall stick'. Impulsively, she threw the coat on to the sofa and flung her arms around Bart. 'I like you just the way you are,' she said, hugging him tightly. 'I didn't realise that you were so sensitive about your height. Or the length of your nose.' She smiled and ran one finger down the centre of his nose. 'I think that's just right, too. I'm sorry I was so tactless the other day. Please don't go away again.'

Bart put one arm round her and smoothed her hair with his other hand. 'I'm not that sensitive about either, and that's not the reason I left,' he said softly. 'I think you know that.'

'Yes, but I still don't know why you did,' Kelsey replied. Bart did not explain. He continued his delicate stroking of Kelsey's hair, his eyes wandering slowly over her face. He really did, she thought dizzily, have the most beautiful, mesmerising, grey eyes she had ever seen. When they flickered with those deep silver lights, as they were doing now, she felt as if she were falling headlong into a pair of huge diamonds. 'Are—are you going to tell me why?' she stammered, trying to regain more solid ground.

Bart smiled, the flickering lights turning into a shower of sparks between the frame of lines that fanned out from the corners of his eyes. 'I'll tell you all about it . . .' he bent and planted a quick, firm kiss on her lips '. . . some time soon.'

The aftermath of Bart's brief, unexpected kiss rocketed through Kelsey like a shockwave that set the entire room swaying as if an earthquake had struck. She clung to Bart and looked quickly towards the prism which hung in her window. It was still. 'Good heavens,' Kelsey said. Then she looked up at Bart, who was watching her with a quizzical little smile curving his lips, and shook her head. 'I thought there'd been an earthquake,' she said. 'I wonder what that means.'

'Maybe that we'd better be careful?' he suggested. 'Forces like that can be dangerous.' He released Kelsey abruptly, then picked up his coat and hung it in her coat cupboard himself.

Kelsey sighed. Bart was right, of course. For the second time it was obvious that physical contact between them set off a powerful reaction, and it was best not to let things get too far off-balance before they were more ready to cope with it. She had to remind herself that she had known Bart for only a few days. It seemed as if she had known him forever.

She watched Bart finish his chore and turn towards her, his broad shoulders so invitingly strong, his smiling mouth so warm and gentle. Some time soon, Kelsey mused as her heart beat faster, she was going to have to send him a clear signal that she was ready for a little more danger! She smiled and held out her hand to him. 'Come with me while I try to clean Elwood up a little. My nieces almost loved him to death and tried to feed him chocolate cake, besides. How did your Easter go? Was it the way you expected?'

Bart looked at her hand warily for a moment, then grasped it tightly and smiled apologetically. 'I'm sorry if I seem ill at ease,' he said, 'but I've had several different problems to cope with in last couple of days, and I'm not sure I've quite resolved everything yet. As to Easter, it was a bit more than I expected. Maybe you'd better sit down while I tell you about it. After what happened this afternoon, I'd have been here tonight whether you wanted me or not.' He picked up Elwood and then handed him back to Kelsey after she sat down.

'Good heavens, what happened?' Kelsey asked, watching as Bart wound his long length backwards around another chair.

He smiled wryly. 'The scene at the Malone Easter celebration was even crazier than usual. It's too bad that you couldn't have seen it. It seems that Ford had found out about your threat to marry me. Right after my father had proposed the usual toast to the continued good health and prosperity of the family, Ford got up and proposed another toast. He'd obviously had too much to drink, but that didn't dampen the effect very much. He raised his glass in my direction and offered a toast to me and my future bride.'

Kelsey gasped and dropped the towel with which she was trying to fluff Elwood's damp fur. 'He didn't!' she exclaimed. When Bart nodded, she shook her head. 'How awful for you,' she said sympathetically. 'I suppose your mother had a fit.'

Bart chuckled. 'Not right away. For some reason,

she thought he meant Fiona Whittington. She jumped up and said how wonderful it was, and why had I kept it a secret? Then Ford interrupted her and told her that it wasn't Fiona at all, it was a cute blonde named Kelsey Cameron. Then everyone, which was about twelve people, as I recall, stared at me and said in a sort of Greek chorus, "Who is Kelsey Cameron?"'

Bart laughed outright. 'I'd give anything to have a videotape of that moment,' he said. 'I was trying so hard to figure out what it must mean if Ford knew about you, that I was paying very little attention to the other implications that had everyone else so excited. When I didn't answer the chorus, my father roared out, at about ninety decibels, "Who the hell is Kelsey Cameron?" That woke me up, and I suddenly remembered that my father knew your stepfather, so I answered, "She's Donald McMurphy's stepdaughter". That seemed to set Ford off again and he yelled even louder, "Who in hell is Donald McMurphy?"' Bart paused and chuckled, shaking his head in bemusement. 'My mother said, "Wasn't he that handsome policeman who came to our wedding?" and my father said that yes, he was, and he was also the finest detective that the Police Department ever had, and how did I ever happen to meet his stepdaughter? Right about then, Ford excused himself and I spent the next few minutes trying to do some fancy footwork around the questions.'

'Oh, I do wish you'd had a videotape of that, too,' Kelsey said, shaking her head. 'It sounds like something straight out of a night-time soap opera. How on earth did you manage to get out of there alive? Or is this a ghost I'm talking to?'

Bart smiled ruefully. 'No, I'm still here. I managed to neither confirm nor deny that we're getting married, but my mother isn't happy about it, even though I told her quite plainly that Fiona and any like her have less chance than the proverbial snowball in hell. I also avoided any mention of what we're really up to, but——' he raised his eyebrows meaningfully at Kelsey, his expression now very sober, '—I'm sure that Ford suspects. I'm also sure that he's deeply involved in the whole nasty business. I've thought for some time that he might be, but I didn't want to believe it. I was going to confront him this afternoon, but fortunately he'd gone.'

'Fortunately?' Kelsey questioned.

'I was too angry,' Bart said with a grimace. 'And I don't want to make accusations without facts to back them up. I at least owe him that much.' He stared glumly at the floor, and Kelsey's heart went out to him again.

'You think a lot of your brother, don't you?' she said softly.

'*Thought*,' Bart corrected, without looking up. 'When we were kids I worshipped him. He's three years older than I. He was athletic, handsome, gregarious, always the centre of fun. I was the tall, shy stringbean with his nose in a book. I never saw the dark side of Ford's lack of ambition, his willingness to bend the truth and use other people to his own ends. I still don't think it needs to be that way.'

Kelsey frowned. 'What do you mean?'

Bart looked up at her and smiled wryly. 'Why should it turn out that all virtue resides in those who work their tails off eighteen hours a day, while those who have fun instead are only pretty shells? Can't there be a happy medium?'

'I'm sure there can,' Kelsey answered. She wanted to go on, and say that she would be happy to help him look for it, but knew that he might not be in the mood for that just now, with the bitter suspicion about his brother in the forefront of his mind. Instead she held up the now cleaner Elwood and looked into his face searchingly. 'Perhaps, if we consult this magical rabbit, he can help us find the way,' she said. She pretended to whisper something into the rabbit's ear, then to listen attentively to what the rabbit whispered into hers. She nodded. 'Elwood says,' she said to Bart, 'that it is time that we gave our brains a rest for a few minutes and had some of that chocolate cake my mother sent home with me. He had a lot of that earlier, and recommends it highly.'

Bart looked at Kelsey strangely, then suddenly his expression cleared and he laughed outright. 'Sometimes I forget that you're a schoolteacher,' he said. 'You do those things so naturally. It's great. I'll bet the children love you.'

Kelsey felt a little tugging sensation inside her chest, as if something were pulling on her heart. Bart thought her schoolchildren must love her, but could he imagine himself loving her, too? Quite suddenly, she knew that she hoped with her whole heart that he could. 'At least they don't throw things at me,' she said with a modest little shrug. 'I hope you don't think I'm treating you like a child.'

Bart shook his head. 'Not at all. I hope you don't think I was being critical. I'm just not used to a person being as spontaneous and whimsical as you are. I love it.'

That, Kelsey thought, feeling a warm flush come to her cheeks, was closer than she'd hoped. She put Elwood down very carefully on a chair. Maybe he was a little magical, at that. 'Cake?' she asked, looking at Bart.

'Yes, ma'am. Please,' he replied, nodding.

Kelsey brought them each a plate, cut the cake, and then put the container of icing on the table between them. 'Help yourself to the extra icing,' she said with a smile. 'My mother thought I deserved some, since I didn't get to lick the bowl like I used to. I think it's a good idea that I may keep using from now on. I always seem to run out of icing before I do cake.'

'Definitely a good idea,' Bart agreed. He looked at Kelsey thoughtfully. 'I've always noticed that I run out of chocolate sauce before the ice-cream is gone, too. From now on, I'm going to ask for an extra supply of it. I think most people take what's given to them far too often without complaining, don't you?'

Kelsey shook her head. 'I refuse to discuss it. You're supposed to be resting your brain and instead you're turning a piece of cake into a serious philosophical discussion.' Impulsively, she dipped her finger into the chocolate icing and drew a streak across Bart's cheek with it.

For a moment, Bart looked completely taken aback. Then his eyes flashed silver daggers. 'Watch out, Kelsey,' he warned, dipping his own finger into the icing. 'This is war!' He smeared a sugary blob down her nose.

Astounded, Kelsey stared at him, wide-eyed. Then she responded to the gleam in Bart's eyes. 'Oh, is it now!' she said, loading her forefinger again with the delectable, sticky stuff. She lunged towards Bart, but he dodged, laughing, and caught her wrist.

'Lick off your finger,' he demanded, bending her arm back towards her.

'No!' Kelsey said, her heart racing even as she shook her head vigorously. Bart was handsome enough at any time, but when he got that wild, devilish gleam in his eyes he was the most exciting man she had ever met. She smiled shyly at him. 'You captured me, you disarm me,' she said. 'Lick it off yourself.'

Bart looked down at Kelsey's finger, the tip of his

tongue circling the inside of his lips. He flicked a knowing glance at her from beneath lowered lashes, then very deliberately raised her hand towards his mouth. Slowly, he began licking the chocolate from her finger, his eyes fixed intently on hers.

Nothing in Kelsey's experience had prepared her for the kind of arousal that Bart's tantalising tongue on her fingertip sent rushing through her. She felt weak, her arms and legs tingling. Waves of longing coursed through her body, her breathing shallow, her lips parted, as she watched, fascinated, the smouldering, fiery darkness of Bart's eyes, and felt the soft moist warmth of his tongue. By the time that he had finished, she felt as if she were lost in another universe, one that was dominated completely by a pair of grey eyes that saw into her very soul.

Bart continued to hold her hand next to his lips, nibbling at it with little kisses, while their eyes held and, in the intensity of that look, exchanged a deep understanding of how strongly they were both aroused. Kelsey thought that she now saw in Bart's eyes a new fire, a slightly arrogant gleam, that spoke of a man who felt powerful with a woman whom he knew responded to him. It sent another thrill of excitement through her. She wanted him to feel that way, even though it might be dangerous.

At last he lowered her hand and placed his other hand over it, possessing it completely. Although he spoke calmly, there was a deep, sensual warmth to his voice as he asked, 'Now, how am I ever going to convince you that I came over here to spend the night for only the most noble of reasons?'

CHAPTER FIVE

SPEND the night? Kelsey swallowed hard. Bart had obviously received the message that she was ready for some degree of dangerous intimacy, but she wasn't sure at all of what degree. 'Spend the night?' she said aloud, her voice a tiny squeak. She tried desperately to get her whirling mind to work. She sincerely doubted that Bart was any more interested in one-night stands than she was. But why did he want to stay? She smiled faintly at him, then cleared her throat noisily. 'That's right. You never did tell me . . . why it was you'd decided you had to come over here this evening. It wasn't just to get away from everyone hassling you?'

'Of course not,' Bart replied, looking amused at Kelsey's obviously nervous response. 'I could have gone home and done that.' He dropped his eyes beneath their fan of thick, dark lashes and caressed the back of Kelsey's hand with his fingertips. 'I'm afraid,' he said, looking back at her face, 'that Ford may try to make trouble for you . . . and me, too, of course. I don't know what he might do, but I don't want you here alone.'

'I see.' Kelsey licked her lips nervously. It was time that she told Bart about Ford's visit, but she hated to do it. It would probably make him more angry with Ford than ever.

'What is it, Kelsey?' Bart asked. He leaned forward and peered anxiously into her face. 'You can trust me. Believe me, I would never . . .'

'I know you wouldn't,' Kelsey interrupted quickly. 'I do trust you, almost . . . completely. It's just that . . .' She took a deep breath and heaved a sigh. She did not feel, at the moment, like starting an argument with Bart about whether he was going to spend the night or not. She had better get her wits about her before she did that. So, instead of pursuing that topic, she suggested, 'Let's clean up our faces, finish our cake, and then go into the living-room. I think it's time we put everything we know together and came up with some theory to operate on. That's what Rake Devlin would do now. That is, if you want to go on and try to figure out this case, after all.'

'Good idea,' Bart agreed. 'Have you got some paper so that we can write things down as they occur to us?' He raised his eyebrows questioningly, and then grinned at Kelsey's reproving look. 'I guess that's a stupid question to ask a schoolteacher, isn't it?'

'It certainly is,' she replied.

A few minutes later, Kelsey and Bart were seated at her round oak table, each with a pad of paper and a pencil. The case descriptions that Bart had left behind were on the table between them. 'I read those over after you left on Friday,' Kelsey said. 'I was going to ask my stepfather what ideas he might have, but then I decided not to, since you didn't want to go on with it. Now I wish I had.'

'We can ask him later,' Bart said. 'Let's see what we come up with first.' He picked up the papers and glanced through them. 'Doesn't it seem odd to you that in every case there was a second person who disappeared after the accident?'

Kelsey nodded. 'I noticed that, too. Almost as if they were accomplices. Robert Santos mentioned that there was a man who pounded his hand with his fist, too. Do you suppose the poor man was only *supposed* to get a broken finger?'

'Could be,' Bart agreed. 'The question is, if the accidents were all set-ups, who arranged them and how did they get the people to participate?' He looked at Kelsey questioningly.

That, Kelsey thought, looking down and doodling on her pad of paper, was a rather strange question for Bart to ask her. Her letter to him, signed Joe Rocco, had made one suggestion that still might be viable. Of course, she hadn't mentioned in the letter her 'third party', the playboy from her story, who could be Ford Malone. Was that what Bart was driving at?

'It seems to me,' she said slowly, 'that Joe Rocco's idea might still be the answer. There is a lot of illegal gambling around town, and if people get in debt and don't have the money to pay, the underworld bosses or whoever is in charge can get pretty nasty. However, there could be someone else involved as a go-between, so that the mob doesn't look like they're involved. Is that what you're driving at?' She thought she saw a flicker of admiration in Bart's eyes as he nodded, although his expression was grim.

'That's exactly it,' he replied, scribbling some notes on his page.

'I can't see how that explains Morris Carter's role,' Kelsey said, watching him, 'and if you think that your brother is involved, why would he want to target your own stores? That doesn't make any sense to me.' She stopped and looked at Bart, hoping that he would go on from there, and she would not have to say anything more about his brother just yet.

'Why, indeed?' Bart said drily. He hunched his broad shoulders and tapped his pencil on the paper before him. 'I expect,' he said slowly, 'that there is someone who knew that all the supposed victims were in debt. That person also knew that Morris Carter is not above taking questionable cases, because he's been around a lot of sleazy operations and knows who such people are. That person is probably my brother.' Bart paused and drew a little tree diagram on his paper, with lines connecting the various people to each other and the Big Winner stores. He stared at the diagram and shook his head. 'Why?' he repeated.

'It doesn't explain, either,' Kelsey put in, 'what good it would do to go to all that trouble unless there were some guarantee of results. Someone inside the insurance company, such as the claims adjuster. How could they have been sure about that?'

'Insurance investigators aren't necessarily saints, either,' Bart said drily. 'If Ford knew something about one of them . . .' He reached for the case descriptions and looked through them quickly. 'The same person investigated every one. He kept the amounts relatively small, so the company probably thought he was doing a great job.' Bart looked at Kelsey, his eyes lighting with an apparent revelation. 'That could be it. That could be the answer!' he exclaimed.

'It certainly could,' Kelsey agreed. 'Your brother could have figured that the stores were an easy mark, and helped set up the accidents for a percentage of the claims. Do you think he'd do that to his own family, just for the money?'

'If he needed the money,' Bart said darkly. He made an unpleasant sound. '*Especially* if he needed the money. He's never felt that his share of the family funds was adequate, in spite of the fact that he does virtually nothing to earn them.' Bart leaned back in his chair, his face grim. 'My guess is that Ford has gotten himself in debt to some of the big boys in Las Vegas. The kind that are very unpleasant about unpaid debts. He knows better than to come to me or Dad for money. This is a great way to get even with us for being so stingy.'

'I'm afraid that makes a lot of sense,' Kelsey said sadly, 'but how do you plan to find out if it's true?'

Bart leaned back and looked at Kelsey thoughtfully. 'I think we probably ought to make a trip to Las Vegas,' he said. 'I've got a pretty good idea who the people are that Ford might have had dealings with.'

'To Las Vegas?' Kelsey asked, rather surprised that Bart intended to track his idea directly to its possible source. 'What would we do there?'

'Check around and see if I'm right about Ford being in debt.' At Kelsey's worried look he smiled. 'I think all I'd have to do is put out the word that I'm going to pay off anything he owes, so that he can make a fresh start.'

'Aren't you apt to get claims from all kinds of people there, too, if you do that?' Kelsey asked, sceptical of Bart's plan.

'Don't worry, I'll require proof,' Bart replied. 'Let's see . . .' He rubbed his neck in a characteristic gesture. 'I have some business to attend to here, first. How about going next Friday? We can stay over a couple of nights and have some fun, as well as playing detective.'

'We can?' Kelsey stared at Bart, who seemed quite pleased with his idea. Somehow, she hadn't thought of him as a person who would enjoy the gambling casinos, especially since he described himself as someone who kept his nose to the grindstone eighteen hours a day. 'Do you like to gamble?' she asked.

'Not for high stakes,' Bart replied, 'but I like to play a little blackjack and see the shows once in a while. Do you like Las Vegas?'

'I haven't been there in years,' Kelsey confessed. 'The last time I went, I was too young to do anything but watch my mother play the slot-machines.'

'Then it's time you did go,' Bart said decisively. 'It's an interesting world.' He looked at his watch. 'Maybe I'd better turn in. I have a managers' meeting at eight in the morning. If you just give me a blanket and a pillow, I'll sleep on the sofa.'

Kelsey frowned. Just because Bart knew that she was strongly attracted to him, he didn't need to think he could be so bossy. 'I don't think you need to stay,' she said. 'Even if your brother does think we're likely to discover what he's up to, I can't believe he would do anything drastic to me.'

'I doubt it, too, but I don't want to find out the hard way that I'm wrong,' Bart said firmly. 'Now, are you going to co-operate or do I have to tear this place apart to find a blanket and a pillow?'

'My goodness, you can be bossy!' Kelsey said, scowling at him. 'I hate to bring up your height, but you are definitely too tall for that little sofa of mine. You take my bed, if you insist on staying. I've slept on the sofa lots of times, sometimes just because I've fallen asleep watching TV. It's very comfortable for me.'

Bart looked round the room and then towards the door to Kelsey's bedroom. 'All right,' he said, 'but I want the door to the bedroom left open so I can hear anything that happens out here.'

'Suit yourself,' Kelsey said, shaking her head at Bart's determination. If she didn't feel that she already knew him quite well, she would think that he was using the supposed threat from Ford in order to stay the night. But how, she wondered, was he going to handle tomorrow night, and the nights after that until the case was resolved? He had better not have any ideas about moving in with her. As it was, the neighbours were probably going to be at least mildly curious about the man who had parked his Mercedes in front of her apartment all night.

At that thought, Kelsey made a detour on her way to find her extra pillows and peered out between the blinds in her bedroom window. There was no car in front of her apartment at all! 'Where did you park?' she asked Bart, as she tossed the pillows on to the sofa. 'I don't see your car.'

'I had Henry drop me off,' Bart replied with a knowing little smile. 'I thought it would be better all around if I didn't telegraph my presence.'

An idea which probably delighted the matchmaking Henry, Kelsey thought wryly. She looked at Bart, who had kicked off his shoes and was sprawled in her armchair, glancing through the newspaper. 'You must have been pretty sure I'd let you stay,' she remarked. She felt a minor earth-tremor from the gleam in Bart's eyes as they smiled at her over the top of the newspaper.

'I could always have called Henry to come and get me,' he said.

But you didn't think you'd have to, Kelsey thought, looking quickly away. She tucked a sheet across the sofa cushions, followed by a blanket, then fluffed her pillow and set it in place. When she returned from getting into her nightdress, dressing-gown and slippers, Bart was still calmly reading the paper. 'You can retire now,' she said, trying to sound coolly distant. 'The facilities are all yours and I've even turned your bed down.'

'Thank you,' Bart said. He put the newspaper down and looked at Kelsey, a slow smile spreading across his face and lighting an even more intense glow in his eyes. 'You look like an angel in that pink garment,' he said. Then he sighed and got to his feet. 'If I had Ford's technique,' he said, 'we'd both be sleeping in your bed tonight.'

'Oh, no, we wouldn't,' Kelsey said tightly. 'If you had Ford's technique you wouldn't even be staying here.' When Bart laid his hand along her cheek, she caught it and held it away from her. 'Bart,' she said huskily, 'just go to bed. Please.'

'All right,' he said, his voice so low that Kelsey could barely hear it. But he did not move, and his fingers curled round her hand and held it tightly.

For a long time they stood there, motionless, their eyes riveted together. I wanted a little more danger, Kelsey thought, the sound of her own pulse pounding in her ears. But this may be too much. I want him more than I've wanted any man since . . . Kelsey tore her hand free and shook her head. 'Goodnight, Bart,' she said hoarsely.

'Goodnight, Kelsey,' he replied. He turned and walked to her coat cupboard and took out his trenchcoat.

'Wh-where are you going?' Kelsey asked, her heart plummeting into her stomach at the thought that Bart was now leaving her again.

'Nowhere,' Bart replied. He plunged his hand into his coat pocket and pulled out a dark blue silk packet. 'Travel pyjamas,' he said, holding it up for

Kelsey to see. 'I hate sleeping in my underwear.' He smiled sympathetically at Kelsey's pale face and anxious expression. 'I don't blame you for thinking I'm pretty erratic,' he said, 'but that's not my usual way. When you've known me longer you'll see that I'm a very reliable person, and once I make up my mind to something I stick to it through thick and thin. I promised I wouldn't run out on you again, and I won't. Not ever.' He gave Kelsey a warm smile. 'Sleep well. I'll see you in the morning.'

'Goodnight,' Kelsey said again, then quickly turned out the light and got into her makeshift bed, Bart's promise ringing in her ears as if it were a recording that played itself over and over. 'I won't, not ever. I won't, not ever.' Why, she wondered, did it sound as if somewhere in there were the words 'Till death us do part?'

She pulled her covers up round her ears and closed her eyes, feeling so tense that she was sure she would never get to sleep. She listened to the sounds of Bart getting ready for bed, then the click of the light going off. Devil climbed on to the sofa and curled up next to her feet, purring contentedly. The cuckoo-clock gave eleven chirps, and then all was quiet. So quiet. And safe, because Bart was here to protect her. Kelsey smiled to herself and drifted off to sleep, oblivious to the world until the sensation of a cold breeze blowing across her face awakened her.

For a few seconds, Kelsey did not remember that she was in her living-room instead of her bedroom, nor why she was there. Then it came back to her in a rush that left her shaking with fear. There shouldn't be any breeze unless a window was open! She started to push herself up in order to see over the end of the sofa, but froze part-way. What was that metallic, tapping sound? It sounded like her venetian blinds, hitting against the sill of the window that overlooked the garden at the side. Someone was either in the apartment or trying to get in! But they couldn't have climbed in without either moving the lamp on the table in front of the window or knocking it over. Were they still out there, trying to decide what to do? What was that funny little sound, like sand grating under someone's feet?

Her teeth now chattering with fear, Kelsey continued her silent movement, trying to see over the end of the sofa without being seen. When she could see, her heart almost stopped beating. Silhouetted against her window, in the dim light from the street-lamp, was the figure of a man bending to peer in at the window as he reached in and pushed the blinds aside. Kelsey gasped, then let out a scream and vaulted out of her bed, running towards her bedroom as if pursued by a million devils instead of one terrified cat. She flung herself into Bart's waiting arms. 'A man!' she cried, waving her hand frantically towards the living-room. 'He's coming in the window!'

'Stay here!' Bart ordered. He leapt up and rushed into the living-room.

Instead, Kelsey jumped to her feet again and grabbed her tennis racket which was leaning against the wall by her cupboard door. Even as she did, she heard the sound of running feet outside, the slam of a car door, and a screech of tyres as the car took off down the hill at high speed. She dropped the racket again and flew into the living-room, just as Bart turned on the lights. Seconds later she was in his arms, clinging to him and sobbing.

'Some detective I'd make,' she choked out between

sobs. 'I was scared to death. Was it . . . your brother?'

'I didn't get a good look, but it could've been his car, maybe,' Bart replied, stroking Kelsey's back soothingly. 'Did you leave the window open?'

'No, but I might have left it unlocked,' Kelsey said, melting against the comforting warmth of Bart's body. 'Oh, I'm so glad you were here. I'm so glad you're here now.'

'So am I,' Bart said gruffly. He gathered Kelsey into his arms and sat down with her on the sofa, cuddling her in the curve of his shoulder and nestling his lips against her forehead. 'Your heart's still racing,' he said softly, holding his hand against her chest between her breasts. 'Just try to relax. You're safe.'

Kelsey tilted her head and looked at Bart. 'What would you have done if some stranger had come through the window with a gun?'

'I would have taken his gun away and held him until the police got here,' Bart replied. 'If he'd tried anything else, I would have shot him.'

That, Kelsey thought, was exactly what Rake Devlin would have done, but her fictional detective was an expert at karate. Somehow, though, the quiet confidence that radiated from Bart's face made her believe that he could have done the same. She took a deep breath and smiled. 'I believe you really would have, wouldn't you?' she said.

Bart smiled back, silver lights replacing the dark, sober shadows in his eyes that his near encounter with the intruder had produced. 'You'd better believe it,' he said firmly.

The thought flitted briefly through Kelsey's mind that now that she was safe from the intruder she should be moving from Bart's arms, instead of letting her eyes drift down to the gentle curves of his mouth. But it was such a nice mouth, with clean, definite lines. She had never thought about that before, but she liked that kind better than those where it was hard to tell exactly where the lips began and ended. Bart's chin was nice, too, even now when a tiny bit of shadow had begun to show. She wanted to feel it and see exactly how rough it was. Would he mind? Her fingertips seemed to find their way to Bart's chin of their own free will, stroking delicately back and forth. Kelsey felt Bart's arm tighten round her and she looked up at him questioningly.

'Too rough?' he asked.

'No,' she answered, dizzied by the intense hunger that she now saw in his beautiful, changeable grey eyes. She felt it, too, her body responding to the feel of him through the thin silk of his pyjamas. There was, she realised shamelessly, very little between them, for she had nothing on but a thin cotton nightie with bare shoulders like a camisole. Bart's hand was still between them, in a carefully neutral position. If she moved just a little, if she slid her hand behind his neck . . .

She did so, and Bart responded instantly. His mouth covered hers with passionate possessiveness and his hand first cupped her breast, then slid inside her nightie, his thumb and forefinger massaging the hardened peak until Kelsey moaned softly at the wild sensations of pleasure that spread through her body. She pressed eagerly against Bart, losing herself in a world of sensual messages. His tongue teased inside her lips, the hand that held her close pulled her even closer, letting her feel the hard response that was building to match her own longing. They tried to stretch out against each other but the sofa was too short. Somehow they rolled off on to the floor, Bart clutching Kelsey against him protectively. Now, their hands were free to explore more fully, and Kelsey stroked Bart lovingly, shimmers of electricity surging through her at the deep sounds of pleasure that he made. He took her hand away and held it with one hand, while with the other he pushed the top of her nightdress down, his head raised so that he could first feast his eyes on her soft, full curves and then make love to them with his lips. The waves of desire grew almost unbearable until at last Kelsey took hold of Bart's head between her hands and lifted it, seeking his mouth once more with hers. Bart threw his leg across her, moving against her, his skin now bare against hers. She caught her breath in a little whimpering moan as his hand slid upwards along the inside of her thigh and then stopped.

'Oh, lord, Kelsey,' he rasped hoarsely, 'are we ready for this?'

Kelsey opened her eyes and looked into his, trying to make the world stop reeling around her long enough to understand what he was saying. Ready? She had never been so ready! 'Good lord, yes,' she replied.

Bart smiled crookedly and let his hand move on up, to rest on Kelsey's bare tummy. 'That's not what I meant,' he said softly. 'I don't have any protection. Do you?'

Kelsey shook her head. 'No.' She took a deep breath and tried once more to regain a firmer grip on reality. 'I . . . I haven't needed any in . . . such a long time.'

'Neither have I,' Bart said with a grimace. 'And I didn't think I would tonight.' He pulled the bottom of Kelsey's nightdress back down and started to push the top up. 'Maybe I'd better let you do that,' he said. 'I might get distracted from my good intentions, and I'm not sure how many more times I can persuade myself to be noble.'

'Nor me,' Kelsey said, slipping her straps back on, then quickly getting up and reaching for her dressing-gown. As she put it on, she said wryly, 'I don't think I get even one noble to my credit. You must think . . .' She stopped, blushing furiously at the realisation that Bart could very well think almost anything of her after that recent scene. 'If this isn't a stupid time to get around to blushing, I don't know what would be,' she mumbled. 'I'm sorry. I'm very ashamed of myself.' She looked up at Bart, who was now standing beside her, a towering, blue-clad giant with tousled hair and an expression that was somewhere between lost little boy and triumphant caveman.

'I guess I could be ashamed, too, but I'm not,' he said, 'and I don't think you should be, either. We're two adults with a very strong attraction to each other. I don't think it's a question of being ashamed about what we feel or what we're going to do about it. I think it's more a matter of when. Believe me, from now on I'm going to be prepared all of the time, because sooner or later the right time will happen along.'

Kelsey frowned. 'Well, I'm not sure it will. I mean, you don't want to get married, and I don't plan to either . . .'

'Shhh!' Bart put a finger firmly against Kelsey's lips. 'This is no time for a discussion of all eternity. It's time to get some sleep.' He went over to the still open window, closed it and locked it firmly. 'I doubt that we'll have any more company tonight, but I'll be glad to sleep out here if you'd rather I did.'

'No. I . . . I'll be all right,' Kelsey replied. 'Goodnight . . . again.' She watched Bart go into her bedroom, remembering that the last time she had assured him she would be fine she had already known that something out of the ordinary had happened when they met. This time she was sure that she could still be standing on this spot when all eternity rolled round and she would still feel the same. She would still be falling in love with Bart Malone.

CHAPTER SIX

'THAT'S right, tomorrow at ten o'clock instead of today at eight. Thanks, Trudi.' The sound of Bart's voice speaking with authority awakened Kelsey in the morning. He looked across at her sitting up, blinking sleepily, her covers clutched tightly around her. 'Sorry I wakened you,' he said, smiling at her. 'I needed to call my secretary and get that managers' meeting changed. It's already seven-thirty, and I hate to rush in the morning.'

For a moment, Kelsey did not have the slightest idea what Bart was talking about. There seemed to be something she recalled about his having a meeting this morning, but not at seven-thirty. 'Your secretary is in by seven-thirty?' she said, surprised.

'No, I called her at home,' Bart replied. 'She has two little kids, so I knew she'd be up. And now I can take my time getting dressed and we can have coffee and discuss what we should do between now and Friday.'

'Friday?' Kelsey said vaguely. She was not at her best in the morning, and being greeted with the disturbing sight of Bart, still in his pyjamas, did nothing to make her more alert.

'We're going to Las Vegas, remember?' he replied.

'Oh, yes.' Two days in Las Vegas, alone, with Bart. Kelsey felt beads of perspiration form on her upper lip. Should she risk it? More to the point, perhaps, could she afford it? It would not be a good idea to let Bart pay for everything. He might think . . . at

111

least her mother had always said that a man would . . . Kelsey cleared her throat uncomfortably. 'I'm not so sure I ought to go,' she said slowly. 'It could be pretty expensive.'

Bart frowned. 'I hope you don't think I wanted you to pay your own way,' he said in scolding tones. 'I should be paying you extra for helping me. You're already risking life and limb on my behalf. I certainly don't expect you to risk your bank account, too.'

Kelsey could think of no immediate response to dispute Bart's logic. She needed some coffee to get her brain working again. The last part of the night she had tossed and turned, frustrated and confused. Bart, she noticed, looked as if he could have used more sleep himself.

'Why don't you go ahead and get dressed?' she suggested. 'I'll start some coffee.'

'Good idea,' he agreed.

While Bart showered, Kelsey put on her dressing-gown, started her automatic coffee-maker, and then went back to fold up the bedding from the sofa. Bart's shoes were still on the floor next to her armchair. They were, she thought, the biggest shoes she had ever seen. She poked her foot into one of them experimentally, and almost laughed out loud. A shoemaker could make her two pairs of shoes from one of his. She finished folding the bedding, and had just set the pile on the foot of her bed when there was a knock on her door.

'Oh, great! Now what?' she muttered, running her fingers nervously through her hair. She probably looked perfectly awful. Maybe it was just some salesman whom she could quickly send away. She peered through the peephole. It was a woman, tall, with well-groomed, greying hair and a carefully

made-up face. Probably a cosmetic salesperson,
Kelsey decided. She opened the door a crack without
removing the security chain. 'Yes?' she said politely.

'Miss Cameron?' said the woman, fixing Kelsey
with a critical look from a pair of direct, grey eyes.

Oh, good lord, Kelsey thought, her stomach going
into a knot. Those grey eyes looked only too familiar.
For a few seconds, Kelsey's mind freewheeled,
darting from one ridiculous thought to another. In
the end, her natural honesty prevailed and she
nodded dumbly.

'I'd like to talk to you, Miss Cameron,' the woman
said then. 'I'm Olivia Malone, Bart's mother.'

Good heavens, she couldn't let her in! Kelsey
licked her lips nervously. 'I—I'm not dressed,' she
stammered. 'If you could come back . . .'

'I'm a very busy woman, Miss Cameron, and I
don't mind at all if you're in your bathrobe. Please,
let me come in.' She smiled cajolingly. 'I really do
think we should have a little talk, don't you?'

'Well . . . all right,' Kelsey said. 'Just a minute. I'll
have to close the door so I can get the chain off.' She
closed the door, then ran frantically to the bathroom
door and poked her head inside. This was no time
to worry about privacy! 'Your mother's here,' she
hissed. 'Stay put!' Then she flew back, took off the
chain, and opened the door. 'Do come in and sit
down, Mrs Malone,' she said breathlessly. 'I'll have
some coffee ready in just a minute.'

'Thank you,' said Olivia Malone graciously. She
looked around Kelsey's sunny living-room. 'Pleasant
place you have,' she said, taking a seat on the sofa.
'Have you lived here long?'

'About five years,' Kelsey replied, perching
nervously on the edge of her armchair. 'Since I

started teaching at the elementary school. I teach fifth grade.'

Mrs Malone raised her eyebrows. 'I didn't realise that teachers were paid well enough to afford this neighbourhood.'

'They can't,' Kelsey said quickly, without thinking. Then she blushed furiously. 'I—I have a little extra income,' she said. Which, she quickly realised, sounded even worse. 'From my late father's estate,' she invented.

'Oh, yes,' Olivia Malone said, frowning. 'You're Donald McMurphy's stepdaughter, aren't you? I don't recall you being in the picture when he attended my wedding. But then you'd have been quite small.'

Kelsey smiled wryly. 'I wouldn't have been here at all, Mrs Malone,' she said. 'I'm only twenty-eight. My father died when I was fifteen, and Donald and my mother were married when I was eighteen.' She watched Olivia Malone digesting that information, wondering when it was that the woman was going to stop making small talk and get to the point of her visit. Perhaps if she offered her some coffee . . . 'I believe the coffee is ready now,' she said. 'Do you take cream or sugar?'

'Black,' Mrs Malone replied, and Kelsey escaped to the kitchen, hoping that coffee would do something to calm her fraying nerves. The sight of Bart sitting at the kitchen table, calmly drinking coffee, did not help. She gave him a desperate look, got out a tray and two cups, and carried the coffee back to the living-room.

While Kelsey poured the coffee, Mrs Malone watched quietly. When Kelsey had again sat in her chair, Bart's mother took a sip of her coffee and looked thoughtful. 'I don't know exactly how to put this, Miss Cameron,' she said, 'but I have been trying for a number of years to get Bart interested in marrying one of the young women of our social set. To no avail, as you are probably aware. Now, it may sound strange to you, since this is supposedly a democratic society, and we are certainly not what would be called "old money", but there are some advantages to having marriages between people who are used to the same things, and for whom money holds no particular fascination, if you understand what I mean.'

Kelsey felt something inside her head go 'pop', as if a switch had been turned on which started the fire of her temper instantly simmering. 'Could you possibly mean,' she said with saccharine sweetness, 'that you think I would marry Bart for his money?'

Mrs Malone looked uncomfortable. 'Well, I wouldn't want to put it that bluntly, but Bart is a rather serious person, not the sort to sweep a young woman off her feet with his charm, as his brother Ford is inclined to do. I would find it rather difficult to believe that at the age of twenty-eight you suddenly find him the most fascinating man you've ever met.'

Good lord, Kelsey thought, staring at Olivia Malone. She didn't know her son at all. It was really rather sad. 'I'm sorry to hear you say that,' she said. 'You know, as a schoolteacher I often find that parents don't really know their children very well. I'd suggest that perhaps you have that same problem. I'm afraid you're selling Bart very short, Mrs Malone. I don't think he needs your help in finding a mate. He's quite capable of doing so himself.'

'Well!' Olivia Malone put her coffee-cup down on the table with a loud clatter. 'You are certainly a most outspoken young woman! However, my point remains that I don't believe you would be as suitable . . .'

'Don't bother, Mrs Malone.' Kelsey interrupted, barely able to keep her temper in check. 'If Bart and I should decide that we want to marry, which we by no means have done at this point, we will do so because we have both decided that we are suitable for each other. In the meantime, why don't you devote yourself to finding someone for your other son? From what I've heard, he needs more help than Bart does.'

'I beg your pardon!' Olivia Malone's voice was almost a screech. 'I did not come here to be lectured by a . . . a . . .'

'Schoolteacher?' Kelsey suggested for her, her own voice rising several decibels. 'Why not? That's what I do for a living. And, I might point out, I do not take kindly to having someone come into my home to insult me and warn me away from their son. Is that what you do for a living?'

Olivia Malone's face became quite red, but she said nothing, only staring at Kelsey as if she were seeing a strange kind of creature that she had never met before. Gradually her colour returned to normal. 'I'm just a mother, Miss Cameron,' she said finally. 'I want what is best for my son.' She got to her feet and gave Kelsey a wry, pinched little smile. 'Perhaps we both want that. I hope so.' She got to her feet and went to the door. Kelsey followed behind, bracing herself for an expected parting shot. Instead, Mrs Malone paused and looked down at Kelsey. 'Would you do something for me?' she asked.

'If I can,' Kelsey replied, startled by this change of tactics. 'What is it that you want me to do?'

'Remind Bart that he is supposed to take Fiona Whittington—or someone—to the ballet on Thursday night. He's on the board of directors, and he is expected to be there.'

'All right,' Kelsey agreed, nodding, 'but I'm not sure if I'll see him before then.'

Mrs Malone looked amused. 'Now, now, Kelsey, of course you will,' she said. 'Almost any minute, I expect. Either that, or . . .' she gestured toward Bart's shoes ' . . . Bart is somewhere, wandering around the city, barefoot. Goodbye, Miss Cameron.'

Kelsey was still staring at the shoes when she heard the door of Mrs Malone's car close behind her. She looked round just in time to see Bart's mother give her a little wave as she drove away, and then jerked her head back again at the sound of uproarious male laughter.

'I don't see anything funny about it!' she said, pushing the door shut behind her and standing there, staring, amazed, at Bart coming towards her with tears of laughter running down his cheeks. 'Don't you know what your mother must think of me?' she demanded. 'I'd even put the bedding away, so there was no sign that either of us slept on the sofa! She'll think I'm just a common . . . slut!'

Bart tried to stop laughing. He put his hands on Kelsey's shoulders, then went into another spasm of laughter and had to rub his eyes and forehead vigorously and take several deep breaths to stop. 'You were wonderful,' he said at last, 'and she won't think that at all. She's not that out of touch with the present, and there was nothing common about the way you stood up to her. I think it was a whole new experience for her, and from what I could hear, she almost liked it. Besides, look at it from my point of view. She started out thinking I was a dull fellow who couldn't interest any woman, and ended up thinking I was quite a man. You did more for my stock in a few minutes than I've been able to do in thirty-five years.' He chuckled, then once again broke into deep laughter.

Kelsey shook her head, then gave up and laughed with him. What did it matter that Mrs Malone probably thought she and Bart had spent the night in the same bed? It was worth it to see him so happy. 'Go and put your shoes on and I'll fix you some breakfast,' she instructed him when their laughter had subsided. 'As soon as I get dressed,' she added. 'If you're not in too much of a hurry to get to work?'

'No, there's no rush,' Bart replied. 'Besides, we need to make some plans.'

After a quick shower, Kelsey put on her usual home apparel of jeans and a T-shirt and hurried into the kitchen. 'What kind of plans were you talking about?' she asked, as she sliced some of the ham her mother had sent home with her and placed it in her frying-pan. 'Were you thinking of trying to find out who the local crime boss is that your supposed victims may be in debt to?'

'I suppose we should do that,' Bart said slowly. 'I'm not sure just where to begin on that one. Since I'm fairly well known, it would be hard for me to make enquiries, and I certainly don't want you getting involved with those people.'

'I don't especially want to, either,' Kelsey said, 'but I was thinking that perhaps Donald still has some of his old contacts. Do you want me to ask him?'

'By all means, if you think he wouldn't mind,' Bart agreed. 'He'd have had contacts that it would take us years to develop.'

Kelsey turned over the ham slices and looked up at Bart, who was leaning against the refrigerator, watching her intently and chewing on his lip. That characteristic pose, she knew now, meant that he was about to spring another new idea on her. 'What are you brewing up now in that devious mind of yours?' she asked.

Bart grinned. 'I'm afraid you're getting to know me too well already. I was trying to figure out how we were going to handle the problem of keeping you safe this week, and I think that probably the best answer is for you to come and stay at my house. I've got a good security system, and there are always people around. Henry's already taken a liking to you, and he'll be happy to have you there.'

Only the scent of ham getting a little too brown diverted Kelsey from staring at Bart and wondering whether he had lost his mind or she had. Did he think he owned her now and could move her around like a pawn on a chessboard? She had said that she didn't have much schoolwork to do this week, but that didn't mean she had nothing to do! Besides, staying at Bart's house . . . . It was probably perfectly beautiful, and he'd have a lovely big bed. Oh, gosh, why had she thought of that?

'I—I can't do that,' she said, trying her best to sound calm and reasonable even though her throat felt dry and her hand shook visibly as she removed the ham from the pan and turned down the heat. She started breaking eggs into the pan. 'I have things to do here,' she said. 'I can't just pick up and leave like that! Besides, if your mother thinks something illicit is going on now, what would that make her think?'

'She doesn't live there,' Bart said calmly, 'and there would be no reason for her to know. I was afraid you wouldn't like the idea at first, but seriously, Kelsey, it's the only sensible thing for you to do. This place is extremely easy to break into, day or night, and I don't want to have to worry about you every minute that I'm not with you.'

Kelsey put their plates on the table and tried to think quickly. It was not only her anxiety about her increasingly strong feelings for Bart that made his idea impossible. She had writing she needed to work on, correspondence to take care of, and there was no way that she was going to go off and leave her precious files of manuscripts unguarded. But how on earth was she going to explain all that to Bart, without letting him know her secret or misleading him into thinking that she didn't want his company or appreciate his concern? She knew he was beginning to feel confident that she cared for him, but he didn't have the brash arrogance of a Ford Malone that made him think every female in the world was dying to leap into his bed. If ever she needed her talent for fiction, she needed it now!

'I'm afraid there's no way I can come to your house, Bart,' she said, trying to sound logical and matter-of-fact. 'You see . . . I have a research paper that I have to work on. There's a . . . a professor who asked me to work with him on a study of the . . . er . . . kinds of problems that grade-school children discuss with their teachers, and he just brought me the data on Saturday morning. I've got to do some graphs and then start writing up the results for publication.'

'Bring it with you,' Bart replied. 'There are plenty of places at my house where you can work, undisturbed.'

'Oh, I couldn't,' Kelsey said, shaking her head

firmly. 'I have a whole filing cabinet full of things I need to have at hand. They're not only necessary, they're irreplaceable. I wouldn't dare leave them here, unguarded. Besides, I simply can't work if I'm not in my own special little place. My mind goes blank. Really.' She smiled pleadingly at Bart, who was eyeing her suspiciously. 'It's nice of you to worry about me, but I'll be fine. No one's going to bother me during the day, and I could . . . I could hire a security guard at night. Donald could recommend someone.'

'I can imagine how pleased your parents would be if they thought you were in that kind of danger,' Bart said drily.

'Oh, dear, I suppose that's true,' Kelsey said, biting her lip. 'But then, they would wonder what was going on if I went to your house, and I'd have to let them know where I was. My mother calls several times a week when I'm on holiday.' She frowned and tore a piece of toast in half with unnecessary force. 'Darn it, anyway,' she grumbled. Now that she thought about it, she really wouldn't mind terribly going to Bart's house, but it would cause quite a few problems. She leaned her chin on her hand and watched him finishing off his large breakfast with gusto. It was nice having him here, too. More than nice. She wouldn't mind sharing breakfast-time with him for a lot of mornings in the future, but so far he still seemed more concerned with her safety and with the disposition of the lawsuit problem than with any relationship between them beyond sexual attraction. Which wasn't too surprising, she reminded herself. After all, he did have a tremendously responsible position with the Big Winner stores, not to mention the fact that he had to deal emotionally with having his brother possibly turn out to be the villain of the piece.

Bart looked up and caught Kelsey watching him. 'Terrific breakfast,' he said, smiling at her. 'Good company, too.'

'Better, if I'd go along with your plans,' Kelsey suggested, smiling back at him, 'but I just can't.'

'I've got the answer,' Bart replied, the slightly arrogant gleam in his eyes telling Kelsey that she had at least successfully prevented him from thinking she didn't appreciate his concern. 'I'll have Henry stay here with you during the day. There's not much for him to do at my place, and I certainly don't need him to drive me around. He can bring you to my house at dinnertime, and bring you back in the morning. Between times, I'll have the security company that guards my house send someone over here to keep an eye on things. How will that be?'

Kelsey sipped her coffee and looked into the soft silvery glow of Bart's eyes. She could think of no logical reason for arguing over that plan, but there was a reason, not logically so much as emotionally compelling. Now that she had recovered from her morning torpor and the shock of his mother's visit, she was beginning to feel a reawakening desire to have Bart's arms around her again. He had, she remembered, promised never to be without protection again, anticipating a time when they would surely make love. Could she trust Bart, or herself, to spend that much time together in intimate contact? It was not as if they were engaged, although his mother obviously thought that was her plan, as a result of Ford's announcement. Still . . . she would feel safer from any other threat if she accepted Bart's plan. If there were actually someone who wanted her out of the picture entirely, for some perverse or insane reason, it could quickly become academic whether she and Bart were engaged or ever would be.

'I guess that will work out all right,' Kelsey replied at last. 'My mother usually calls during the day, so I won't even have to make up a story for her.'

'Good!' Bart said, obviously relieved. 'I'll call Henry and tell him to bring the Mercedes over for me. It might be a good idea for you to move your car out in front in case you and Henry want to leave in a hurry. You wouldn't want to find out that someone had disabled your garage door opener, like Rake Devlin did to that fellow in one of Rocco's stories.'

Hurry Up and Kill Me, Kelsey said. 'Did you like that one? I . . .' Kelsey barely caught herself in time. She had almost said that she wrote that scene after her own garage door opener failed to work and jammed her door half-open! 'I thought maybe that was a little too pat,' she said instead. 'But moving my car is a good idea. I'll do it as soon as Henry gets here.'

While Bart made his call, Kelsey sat, nervously knitting her fingers together, oblivious to the fact that she should be clearing the table and loading the dishes into her dishwasher. She had led such a quiet, prosaic life up until now, the thrills and excitement of Rake Devlin and Dawn Daley's adventures being strictly vicarious. It didn't seem quite real, all that had happened in the past few days and continued to happen. Maybe, if she closed her eyes and opened them again, she would find out that it was all a dream. She looked up as Bart returned to the kitchen. He smiled at her and she felt as if the sun had burst into the room at the end of a lightning bolt that shook her from head to toe. That was real. Very real. Could she handle it, whatever it might lead?

'What's wrong, Kelsey?' Bart asked softly, pulling out a chair and sitting down close to her. 'You look worried.'

'I was just thinking,' Kelsey said, giving him a little smile, 'that I'm not used to so much excitement. It all seems so strange. And I was wondering . . .' She stopped, uncertain how to tell him that she was nervous about staying at his house without revealing too much about what she felt for him.

'Go ahead,' Bart encouraged. 'If there's anything I can do to make you feel better I want to do it.'

Kelsey swallowed a painful lump and traced her lower lip with her tongue. All you need to do, Bart Malone, she thought to herself, is sweep me into your arms like a knight of old and carry me away to your castle. Aloud she said, 'You've done a lot already. I did wonder . . . you do have an extra bedroom for me, don't you? I mean, I don't want to put you to any trouble . . .' She blushed and looked down. That sounded so stupid. She was beginning to sound like Miss Prunella Prissyness. She took a deep breath and started again. 'What I meant to say was . . .'

'Kelsey, I know what you meant,' Bart interrupted. 'Of course I have a room for you. I asked you to come to my house to be protected, not attacked. I'll leave you completely alone, if you want me to.'

'Oh, no! I didn't mean that,' Kelsey said quickly. 'I wanted to be sure about the room, but I don't want to go and hide in it or anything like that.' Or did she? Maybe hiding in some room would be the best thing she could do. She was startled when Bart reached over and undid her knotted hands, taking one of hers between his huge hands and holding it close.

'I don't think doing battle with my mother the first thing in the morning was very good for your nerves,' he said with a wry smile. 'Just relax. Everything is going to work out. We'll do some swimming and sailing and take in that blasted ballet on Thursday night and just generally have a good time. We haven't had much time to get acquainted yet, you know. You may find out that I'm as dull as my mother thinks I am, and want to hide in your room with a good book.'

Kelsey gave Bart a sideways glance and then looked away. Maybe a few days ago he might have thought she would want to hide and read a book, but she could tell that he now knew perfectly well that she would not. 'You know better than that,' she stated flatly. 'The only thing I might want to hide from is myself, and I don't know of anyone who's figured out how to do that yet.'

Bart's hands tightened around hers. 'Neither do I, but some of us certainly keep trying for a long time, don't we? I suggest we put an end to that as quickly as possible.'

'How do we do that?' Kelsey asked, looking back at him. He was looking at her so intently that when he did not answer for several seconds she was not sure that he had heard her. Then he looked as if he was about to speak, but shook his head instead.

'I'm not sure,' he said at last, 'but maybe this will help.' He stood up, still holding Kelsey's hand, and then gently pulled her to her feet in front of him and put his arms around her. He smiled that slow, sweet smile that made Kelsey's heart beat faster and almost brought tears of happiness to her eyes. Very carefully his arms folded her close, until she was leaning against him, then with one hand he pressed her head towards him until her cheek was nestled on his broad chest, his hand stroking her hair. 'See?' he said softly in her ear. 'It's nothing to be afraid of.'

'Oh, Bart,' Kelsey whispered, her arms going round him to hold him tightly. It felt so wonderful to be close to him. He seemed to have understood so well her anxieties, and was trying with superb tact to tell her that she needn't be afraid of either his feelings or her own. Could he possibly be trying to tell her that he was falling in love with her, too?

CHAPTER SEVEN

A KNOCK on the door disturbed the dreamlike euphoria that Kelsey began to feel as the seconds ticked by and Bart still held her gently in his arms.

'I think Henry's arrived,' Bart said as Kelsey lifted her head to look at him. 'How do you feel now?'

'Wonderful,' Kelsey admitted. 'How about you?'

'Damned reluctant to leave,' Bart replied with a wide, happy smile. 'But duty calls.' He gave Kelsey a quick kiss and then released her. 'I hope you have a good day, working on that research paper.'

'I'll try,' Kelsey said, although at the moment she was not sure how well she would be able to concentrate. Inside, she felt as if some monumental change had sent her blood surging down new and exciting paths.

Henry was all smiles at what he obviously perceived as progress in the relationship between his employer and Kelsey. After Bart had gone, he moved Kelsey's car and then settled down at her kitchen table with a cup of coffee and the morning paper. She took the opportunity to ask him the question that had been bothering her since he had brought her home from the hospital.

'Tell me, if you can, Henry,' she said, 'how you reached the conclusion that Bart and I should get married before you even knew me?'

Henry's eyes twinkled. 'I knew a lot about you before we met. You can either put it down to some leprechauns whispering in my ear, or to the fact that

127

I used to walk the beat with Donald McMurphy. He's still a very dear friend of mine, although I don't see him as often as I'd like. Perhaps you've heard him mention Henry Connors?'

'Of course I have!' Kelsey shook her head. 'I sometimes wonder if there's anyone in this whole huge city that Donald doesn't know. You retired from the police force after you were wounded, didn't you?'

'That's right. My wife decided it was more danger than she cared to live with, with the little ones to think of, so I reluctantly agreed to go along. I would have had restricted duty, anyway, after that.' He lifted his trouser-leg slightly and revealed an artificial limb. 'But don't you worry, Miss Cameron,' he added. 'I can protect you very well, and I won't hesitate to use force if necessary.'

'I certainly hope it won't be!' Kelsey said fervently. With every passing minute, it seemed, she was getting farther and farther into a re-enactment of one of her stories, where shadowy figures from the past slipped in and out of the present, and no one ever knew who was on which side until the very end. The heroic Henry Connors would, she was sure, be on the side of law and order. The only problem was that in the real *Case of the Crooked Claims*, it still was not entirely clear who was doing what to whom, and why.

'That reminds me.' Kelsey muttered to herself, remembering the phone-call she planned to make to Donald. She flashed a smile at Henry. 'I guess I'd better get to work. I have a paper I'm working on with a university professor. Help yourself to more coffee and anything you find in the refrigerator or cupboards that looks edible.'

'Don't you worry, Miss Cameron,' Henry said, 'I'll get along just fine.'

'Call me Kelsey,' she said with a smile. 'I'm only Miss Cameron to fifth-graders.' Kelsey temporarily felt the usual sense of relief that going into her study and closing the door behind her produced. Then she realised that she was going to have to tell Donald that she was now assisting Bart Malone. It was going to be tricky, trying to explain to Donald what she wanted without revealing too much about what had happened so far.

'How are you and Bart getting along?' Donald asked, after she had managed to convince him that she was acting only in an advisory capacity and that he should call Bart personally if he got any helpful information about local crime figures.

'Very well,' Kelsey said. 'He's a very nice man.' Which, she thought after she had hung up, was the understatement of the year, if not the century. Bart was wonderful, and she adored him!

After her conversation with Donald, Kelsey tried to pull all the fragments of the mystery together as if she were going to turn them into a book, but it was impossible to make it all hang together, especially since her mind kept drifting back to place her once again in Bart's embrace. Maybe, she thought finally, if she went back to her fictional account and started to write, something would occur to her. And, even if it didn't, it would be a lot more fun than tearing up page after page of notes and outlines that got nowhere.

The new approach relieved Kelsey's frustration, although it suggested no brilliant solutions. She was soon absorbed in the creative process. Promptly at five o'clock, Henry knocked on her door. 'We'll be leaving soon,' he informed her. 'The guard is here and Mr Bart's on his way. He said to bring your swimming suit and something comfortable for an evening sail, when it's apt to be a bit cool.'

Kelsey locked her desk and files and quickly sorted through her casual clothing. She put on a pink sweater and slacks because Bart had liked her in pink, packed the required things, and was ready just as Bart arrived at the door.

One look at Bart's tall form ducking his head and coming into her living-room, and Kelsey could scarcely keep herself from running to him and throwing her arms round him. He looked tired, but his smile of greeting was anything but worn. If Henry and the young guard had not been there, Kelsey was quite sure he would have greeted her with a kiss. As it was, he said a simple 'Hello, Kelsey,' and then introduced himself to the guard and gave him firm instructions on staying alert at all times. He had Kelsey travel in front while he drove, joking with Henry that he now not only sat where his employer usually did, but he could deal with all his problems from now on, too.

'Did you have a bad day?' Kelsey asked as they drove southwards near the ocean.

'Not much worse than usual,' Bart replied with a wry smile. 'How about you? Did you make some headway on that paper?'

'Some,' Kelsey answered. 'It took me a while to get into it. There's so much to sort out.' Which was, she told herself to squelch the twinge of guilt she felt at perpetuating a lie, a very good description of exactly what she had been doing.

They made idle conversation as they drove, at last turning off the main road into a hilly area of emerald-green lawns and spacious houses secured by iron fences. At the touch of a button, a gate swung open and Bart drove through, along a winding drive, between lush plantings of begonias and tropical plants, that ended on a hill overlooking the ocean at a house of such strikingly modern design that it took Kelsey's breath away. With its angular siding and the sweep of a roof that rose to two storeys at each end, it looked like a gull that had come in from the sea and alighted on the point of land to watch for passing prey.

'Oh, Bart,' she whispered. 'This is gorgeous. What a view you have, and with all that glass . . .'

'I'm glad you like it,' Bart replied. 'The rest of the family, except for Ford, hate it. Not solid and imposing enough. They'd prefer something that looks like a bank.' He grinned as Henry made a 'Hmmmph' sort of sound. 'That's Henry's opinion of the rest of the family's taste,' he said.

'I think I'll go along with that,' Kelsey agreed, 'if they don't like this place.' She could see that Bart was very pleased at her reaction to his home. 'Did you have a hand in the design?' she asked.

'I gave the architect a sketch,' he replied, 'but, of course, I didn't know exactly what could be done. I'm not an engineer. It turned out much closer to what I had in mind than I thought it would.' He took Kelsey's hand. 'Come on. I'll show you to your room, and then we'll have a swim before dinner. The pool's on the other side of the house, just below the windows of your room.'

'Did you pick out the furniture and colour scheme, too?' she asked as they crossed the huge living-room which comprised the centre section of the house. Its entire back wall overlooked the sea through a wall of glass.

'I guess you could say that,' Bart replied with a chuckle. 'I had a decorator, but I nearly drove her crazy. She didn't like the blue I chose, and didn't want so many plants.'

'I love the plants,' Kelsey said. 'I don't think a person can have too many.' Everywhere there were lush tropical plants, carefully tended, accenting with their exotic shapes and colours the more subdued colours of the rugs and walls. The overall impression was one of sheer luxury and beauty. Kelsey had been carefully saving and investing her royalties, but she could see that she was still a long way off from being able to afford anything like this home. At the end, where Kelsey's room was located, there was a stairway.

'There's a recreation room down there which opens on to a terrace and the steps down to the pool deck,' Bart said, pointing down the stairs. 'Your room is above it.' What Bart called the guest-room was in reality a self-contained suite, with a sitting-room overlooking the pool at the back, a bedroom at the front of the house, and a huge bath and dressing-room with its own mini-kitchen at the end. It was done in shades of blue and white, giving it an airy, clean and fresh look that Kelsey thought delightful.

'I think you'll be comfortable here,' Bart said, at which point Kelsey burst out laughing.

'Comfortable! Bart, I've never stayed in any place as elegant as this before. Your mother was right. This is definitely out of my class.'

'Nonsense,' Bart replied, frowning. 'Try to remember that my father was born in a two-room flat over my grandfather's first store. The only so-called class that we have is what money and hard work can buy. *Sic transit gloria*, and all that. What counts is what's inside.' He tapped Kelsey lightly on the forehead. 'That you can't take away.'

'You're right, of course,' Kelsey said quickly. 'I try to tell my students that. But it is rather overwhelming.'

Bart shrugged. 'I know, but you'll get used to it.' He looked at his watch. 'We'd better get changed if we want to get a swim in before dinner. You do like to swim?'

'Oh, yes. I love to,' Kelsey replied.

'Good. I'll meet you by the pool in a few minutes,' Bart said, then turned and left in rather a hurry.

We're both still a little anxious about this situation, Kelsey thought with a sigh. Was it always so hard when two adults, who were rather used to being alone, found that they might have to make a lot of changes if they followed where their emotions were leading them? Maybe not, if they simply jumped into bed. She looked over at the luxurious bed beneath its softly quilted coverlet and then gave herself a mental shake. 'Enough of that, Miss Cameron,' she scolded herself. 'Get ready to go swimming. Vigorous exercise provides excellent relief for sexual tension.' And, heaven knew, there was enough of that whenever she and Bart were in the same room!

She slipped on the slinky, turquoise-blue swimming suit and matching gauze cover-up that she had bought on Rodeo Drive, and then looked at herself in the mirrored walls of the bathroom. Not too bad, she decided. Thank goodness, one of the ways she had splurged with her royalty money was on some really nice clothes.

Bart was already in the pool when Kelsey arrived, swimming leisurely along on his side, taking only a few glides between turns. She took a quick look at his long, slender, mostly bare body in low-cut striped trunks, and decided she would be wise to keep moving and not think too much about that. She took off her cover-up, walked out on to the diving-board, and called out, 'Ready or not, here I come!'

Bart stopped and stared, then let out a long, low whistle.

'Thank you, sir,' she said, inclining her head graciously. Then she dived into the pool and swam quickly to his side. 'Marvellous,' she said. 'This water is just right. Are you standing up there?' Bart's head and shoulders were well above the water.

'I'm afraid so,' Bart replied with a grin. 'That was a beautiful dive.'

'I did some competitive diving when I was in high school,' Kelsey said. 'I guess it's like riding a bicycle. You don't forget how to do it.'

'I was too tall,' Bart said. 'If I don't hit the water perfectly straight it looks like a geyser has erupted.'

'I can imagine,' Kelsey said. They smiled at each other for what began to seem to Kelsey like a very long time. It felt as if they were standing on the edge of some hidden precipice, with each afraid to take the first step. At last she stopped treading water and sank to the bottom, then came up again. Bart was still staring at her. She shook the water from her hair and face, then put her hand up to her hair and felt it. 'Did my wig come off or something?' she asked.

Bart shook his head. 'No, Kelsey,' he said soberly. 'There's nothing wrong with the way you look. Nothing at all. Shall we do a couple of dozen lengths and then go in to dinner?'

'I'll be lucky to finish one dozen,' Kelsey replied. 'It's been a while.' But, she thought, as she swam back and forth not far away from Bart, if she had a pool like this, she would swim every day. She and Bart did seem to have similar tastes and like many of the same things. She liked their dinner of charcoal-grilled steaks, too, but Bart seemed so quiet and subdued that she suggested afterwards that perhaps he was too tired for the sail that Henry had mentioned.

'No, it will be soothing,' Bart replied. 'It's a nice, quiet night.' An electric cart took them down the hill to a little marina, where a beautiful dinghy and a cabin cruiser were riding at anchor. Bart quickly and efficiently got the boat ready to sail, while Kelsey watched, trying to make mental notes on what he was doing so that she might be more helpful in the future. Once they were under way, they sat back against deep cushions and Kelsey heard Bart sigh deeply as he stretched his legs out before him, one hand on the tiller and the other arm flung across the back of the seat.

'This is lovely,' she said. 'I've never sailed before.'

'It's addictive,' Bart said. 'I sail as often as the weather and my schedule permit.'

Bart was silent again, and Kelsey thought about him, swimming alone, sailing alone. Was he worrying about what it would be like if they took that next big step? She had never before stopped to think whether she preferred being alone or not. It was the way things had worked out, and she enjoyed her life. But sharing it with Bart would be very rewarding, too. Bart caught her looking at him and smiled.

'I'm being dull, aren't I?' he said. 'Here I am, in a romantic setting with a beautiful woman, and I'm not even holding her in my arms.' He held out his arm towards Kelsey and she quickly moved to snuggle against his shoulder.

'That takes care of that problem,' she said, smiling up at him. 'I was wondering why you were so quiet. Are you worried about your stores, or something?'

'No, I'm not worried about anything,' Bart said, rubbing his cheek against Kelsey's curls. 'When I come out here, I like to try to stop thinking about anything at all and just soak up the peace and quiet and beauty. It seems a person spends so much time thinking about what if this and what if that, always worried about tomorrow.'

'You must have to do a lot of planning ahead in your work,' Kelsey commented. 'What exactly do you do that the manager of a single store doesn't do?'

'Planning ahead is a lot of it,' Bart said. 'Keeping up with innovations, maintaining quality, the physical facilities, personnel. Endless detail. Not exactly the stuff of which scintillating conversation is made.'

'But I want to hear about it,' Kelsey said. She lifted her head and smiled mischievously at Bart before she tapped the tip of his nose. 'I want to know what you're doing all of those hours when your nose is to that grindstone.'

Bart gave her a sceptical look. 'You don't seriously want to know that,' he said. 'That is *very* dull.'

'No, it isn't,' Kelsey contradicted him. 'A teacher needs to know things like that. You'd be surprised at some of the questions I got after we visited your store. Now, am I going to get a good explanation, or shall I quiz you?'

'I'll talk,' Bart said, pretending to look frightened. 'I always hated quizzes.' While they sailed for almost an hour down Santa Monica Bay and back, he described his work, his obvious enthusiasm for it impressing Kelsey even more than his vast knowledge.

'You really love your work, don't you?' she said, when they again approached their mooring.

'Most of the time,' he replied, smiling down at Kelsey's upturned face. 'Almost as much as I've loved having you here to tell about it.' He bent his head and kissed Kelsey's lips lingeringly, then quickly released her and leaped to the quay to tie up the boat.

Kelsey watched him, her heart singing an almost triumphant song of happiness. Bart was such a remarkable man. The more she knew about him, the more she loved him. And he had very nearly said that he loved her, too.

'You know,' she said as they returned to the house, 'I'm awfully glad you felt you had to invite me here to protect me. This has been a wonderful evening.'

Bart gave Kelsey a strange look but said nothing until they had parked the cart. Then he took her by the shoulders and turned her round almost roughly to stand in front of him.

'Kelsey,' he said, his eyes intent and serious, 'I would have invited you here to spend time with me and go sailing and do other things with me, even if I hadn't gotten that letter from Joe Rocco. I wanted to get to know you as soon as I met you.' He smiled crookedly. 'I thought I heard bells ringing.'

'Y-you did?' Kelsey stammered.

'I did. It was interesting to find out that you know Joe Rocco, and to be able to work with you in trying to figure out what's involved in those accidents, but that's trivial compared to learning what a wonderful, warm, loving woman you are just being your regular self. I love you, Kelsey. That should be obvious by now.'

'Y-you do?' Tears of both happiness and confusion filled Kelsey's eyes. 'I love you too, Bart,' she said, flinging her arms round him. But what on earth was Bart going to think when he found out that her regular self was both Kelsey Cameron and Joe Rocco?

CHAPTER EIGHT

KELSEY clung to Bart, then suddenly burst into tears which she quickly suppressed when he asked anxiously, 'What's wrong, sweetheart?'

'Nothing.' she replied, smiling up at him through her tears. 'Nothing at all. I'm just sort of . . . overwhelmed with all kinds of feelings.'

'I understand,' Bart said softly. 'I was going to wait and pick a suitably romantic moment to tell you, but it seemed to me that you might have some mistaken notions about how I felt that added to your misgivings about your own emotions. No one wants to be involved in a one-sided love-affair.'

'You don't seem to have been very worried about that,' Kelsey said as she watched, fascinated as always, the interplay of lights and shadows in the grey depths of Bart's eyes. He radiated such quiet strength. She couldn't imagine ever feeling anything but secure and happy as long as she could run to his arms and be held like this whenever she felt anxious or worried.

Bart smiled. 'Oh, I was worried, not so much about whether you loved me but whether you were ready to talk about it and what it may mean for our future. It's a big step for both of us, we've been alone so long. And, of course, you had that tragic loss of your fiancé . . .'

'I can't let that forever keep me from taking any chances on love,' Kelsey said quickly. 'You're right that it is a big step. I was thinking exactly the same thing myself, earlier. But it's . . . almost a relief to be able to tell you that I love you, and go on from there. I guess we did get that hiding from ourselves over with pretty fast, after all.'

'Faster even than I'd hoped,' Bart said. 'Now we can really get to know each other, without a lot of misgivings and questions in the background. I can't imagine even beginning to consider a future together unless we try to be totally honest with each other, can you?'

Kelsey swallowed hard. 'No, I certainly can't,' she agreed. But she was going to have to wait for the right moment to spring her dual identity on Bart. Either he might think it was really terrific, or he might wonder what kind of life she'd had in the past to be able to write those torrid love scenes. Even her mother wasn't totally convinced that she just used her imagination!

Bart sighed, and then hugged Kelsey tightly. 'I guess I might as well admit that I'm relieved, too. I did have a few bad moments when I thought I might have totally misread you. And, of course, the reason I left on Friday night was that I knew, after the way I reacted to seeing you in danger, that my own feelings were far stronger than I was ready to accept so soon. I had to talk to myself very severely to get past that moment of cowardice and realise that I'd be losing the best chance for happiness I'd ever have if I stayed away.'

'I felt as if I'd just lost mine when you left,' Kelsey said. 'I didn't know what to think, or do. It's a good thing I wasn't already sure that I loved you, or I'd probably have run straight down the hill and dived into the first big wave that came along.'

'Poor darling,' Bart said, smiling lovingly at her upturned face. His eyes scanned her face and then rested on her lips.

'You could kiss me now,' Kelsey suggested, feeling

almost breathless with anticipation. 'I think we've talked enough.'

'Not yet.' Bart's eyes flashed with mischief. 'Come on. I have a plan.' He took Kelsey by the hand and led her into the house, now and then looking down at her and grinning like a small boy with a secret. When they were inside the recreation room, he went to the wall and touched a button. At his touch a panel, on a wall which Kelsey had assumed was fixed, moved aside revealing a huge, masculine room done in dark, vibrant colours.

Kelsey gasped in delight. 'Is this your room?'

Bart nodded. 'Come in and look around. I had fun designing a room which could be closed off completely when I want to ignore the outside, or opened up almost completely when I want to feel as if I'm outdoors.' He showed her how other panels moved across the window wall, leaving only clerestory windows high above. There was also a fireplace with gas logs, a wall of bookshelves with an elaborate built-in stereo system, and a comfortable desk. 'I can hole up in here and be a hermit for days when I want to,' he said. He opened the window wall again. 'In case you hadn't noticed,' he said, 'there are no door-frames as such in this house. I don't have to spend my life wondering how many times every day I'm going to crack my head.'

'It's . . . absolutely marvellous,' Kelsey said, trying to take in all the features while, at the same time, Bart's huge bed seemed to be beckoning to her alluringly.

'I thought we might finish out the evening listening to some music,' Bart said. 'It's getting late, but I'm too keyed up to go to sleep yet. How about some Mozart to relax to?'

'That's a great idea,' Kelsey replied, wondering how

the kiss that Bart had refused to give her fitted into his plans. She watched as he closed off the panelled wall, turned on the fire, put on some Mozart symphonies, and then arranged the pile of extra pillows on his bed into an inviting nest.

'Come on,' he said, stretching out against the pillows and patting the place beside him. When Kelsey hesitated he added, 'I promise to be on my best behaviour.' Then his eyes twinkled impishly. 'Or not, if you prefer. I do plan to kiss you very thoroughly, but nothing else unless you want it.'

Kelsey looked longingly at the place Bart had indicated and chewed anxiously on her lip. She felt vaguely foolish and stupid, standing there indecisively. She wanted to make love to Bart, and he knew it, but it was far easier to do so in a moment of passion than actively to decide she was going to. Cowardice. That was what it was. And there was no real reason for it now, except the habit of years of saying no weighing her down. She took a deep breath and smiled at Bart. 'I hope you're ready tonight,' she said.

At the sound of her words, Bart sat up and held out his arms, welcoming Kelsey into them with a groan of happiness. 'Oh, Kelsey, am I ever ready?' he said, before his mouth found hers in a kiss of fiery passion. 'I love you so much.'

The longing that Kelsey had felt whenever Bart held her quickly became an acute, flaming desire. Their tongues explored each other's mouths, their hands eagerly touched and caressed, clothing disappearing almost magically in their mutual desire to be totally close. To Kelsey's surprise and delight, Bart made love with an abandon that she would never have expected from a man who was so careful and meticulous in many respects. His mouth moved down, leaving a trail of burning kisses that covered her breasts and then found their peaks for a long, tantalising time that left Kelsey moaning softly at the surges of pleasure that heightened her desire almost unbearably. It felt as if her skin had caught fire from the kisses that moved down, down, the hands that slowly and gently built her arousal to a pitch she had never felt before. A soft whimper came from her lips at the exquisite touches that sent wild waves pounding through her, flooding every sense until nothing remained but her wanting.

She reached to take Bart's shoulders between her hands and pull him to her, and soared even more dizzily at the darkly naked desire that filled his eyes when he smiled at her and raised himself above her. Carefully, slowly, he entered and possessed her, his eyes never leaving hers as the rhythm built, until at last he closed them at the same moment as Kelsey felt as if the world had shaken violently apart, her body flung high into a turbulent sky and then lowered from the heights by a series of invisible hands that tossed her back, back, back, until once again she lay with Bart on his bed and felt his body covering hers, now quiet and still.

'I love you, Kelsey,' he murmured, turning his head to nuzzle her neck and tease her ear with his tongue. He raised his head and looked down at her, his eyes sleepily warm and still dark with desire. 'Stay here with me tonight,' he said huskily. 'Once isn't going to be enough.'

'Oh, yes,' Kelsey replied, feeling her own longing rekindled by his. She could not imagine ever wanting to be away from the touch of Bart's body next to hers.

For the rest of the night they made love and talked and listened to music, only drifting off to sleep when the first light of dawn appeared. When Bart's alarm went off he groaned and pulled Kelsey close once again. 'I think the Big Winner stores can get along without me today,' he said. 'We could take the cruiser out and spend the day just floating along together. I can send Henry over to guard your treasures and feed the cat. OK?'

'More than OK,' Kelsey replied, stroking Bart's cheek lovingly. 'It sounds heavenly.'

Bart kissed Kelsey and then picked up his bedside telephone and made the necessary calls. 'There,' he said, turning back to Kelsey and taking her in his arms. 'Now we can pretend the rest of the world doesn't exist for a while longer.'

'Are you sure it can get along without us?' Kelsey teased.

'Damned sure,' Bart replied with a chuckle. Then he pretended to look very serious. 'Only for a day, of course.'

They dozed a little more, took a leisurely swim, and then set out on the cruiser, a luxurious boat with a large cabin, complete with a comfortable bed. There was also a galley, its refrigerator laden with champagne and a selection of delectable foods sent down earlier by Bart's excellent cook.

'Oh, how rotten spoilt I'm getting,' Kelsey said as she sat on the afterdeck, eating crab salad, drinking champagne, and watching Bart manoeuvre the boat.

'We'll do some backpacking in the wilderness and get you over it in a hurry,' Bart said, turning to grin at her. 'Right now, I'm going to find a spot to anchor and we'll get out the deep-sea fishing gear.' He found a spot, by what kind of divination Kelsey was not sure, and soon had her hook baited and was just giving her final instructions when something that felt like a whale almost pulled her out of her seat. A short time later,

Bart was roaring with laughter at the scream Kelsey let out when he helped her pull a small hammerhead shark over the side.

'Good lord, it's ugly,' she said. 'Put it back.'

'Gladly,' Bart said. 'He didn't want to stay for dinner, anyway.'

After the fishing gear was put away, Bart gathered Kelsey into his arms and carried her to the cabin for the second time that afternoon. 'You're going to think I'm insatiable,' he said, looking at her with a smile that was at once possessive and hungry with desire.

'You don't hear me complaining, do you?' Kelsey replied. 'Maybe there's some magic in the air. I've never felt like this before.'

'Neither have I,' Bart said. 'Perhaps the magic is us.'

Whatever it was, Kelsey put all thoughts from her mind except the enjoyment of this day of pure pleasure. Once or twice she had a little twinge when she thought that she really ought to tell Bart that he was making love to Joe Rocco, but it was easy to push that notion aside. Why spoil anything so absolutely perfect? Days like this didn't happen very often in a lifetime.

When they returned to Bart's house, Kelsey suggested that perhaps she should sleep in the room that she had been so determined to have, so that Bart could get a decent night's sleep before he returned to work the next morning.

Bart shook his head. 'I'll sleep. I might as well get used to having you with me. I think we should get married, don't you, and as soon as possible? I can't imagine ever wanting to spend time without you again.' As Kelsey stared at him, open-mouthed, he added with a grin, 'That was a proposal, in case you missed it.'

'Oh, Bart!' Kelsey burst into tears and threw her arms around him. 'I—I don't know why I always cry when I'm happy,' she choked out, looking up at him and smiling through her tears.

'Was that a yes?' Bart asked.

'Yes, it was,' Kelsey nodded. 'A definite yes.'

'Oh, Kelsey, my darling love,' Bart said, his own eyes misty as he held her close and kissed her until she was once again dizzy with happiness.

In the morning, Kelsey still felt as if she were flying above the clouds. Bart had suggested she consider their getting married at Las Vegas. 'I want to know that you're really all mine, forever,' he said. 'I know it's soon, but I don't foresee any problems that we can't work out. I'd be willing to wait and have a big wedding, if you want, but I'd feel more comfortable in a small chapel ceremony.' His eyes took on a soft glow. 'And then we could start planning our family.'

'I like that idea,' Kelsey agreed. 'We've made the decision. Why delay? I want to know that you belong to me, too.' She had often wondered whether Tom might still be alive if she and he had got married instead of waiting, as her parents wanted. For he had been driving back to his own home on that fateful night.

During the day, Kelsey tried to think of various tactics for telling Bart that she was also Joe Rocco, famous detective writer. Assorted clever ideas occurred to her, but in the end she decided simply to sit him down after dinner that night and tell him. From everything she knew about Bart by now, she was sure that he wouldn't be upset. He was protective, but he did not try to lord it over her as if he thought she were inferior. He admired her teaching, and her detective skills, such as they were. He would probably be quite pleased to find that she was a successful writer.

When Bart arrived back at her apartment, Kelsey expected to be greeted with a kiss, for he had kissed her goodbye quite passionately in the morning, in spite of Henry's presence. Instead, he only nodded curtly to her and said, 'Let's go. I have a meeting to get to in about an hour. You drive, Henry. We'll let Kelsey out at my house.'

'Good heavens, what's happened?' Kelsey asked, hurrying after him to the car. 'You look as if you've lost your last friend. Is it something to do with those accidents again?'

'Something,' Bart replied, pursing his lips into a grim line.

'Well, tell me what it is!' Kelsey demanded. 'Don't just sit there staring into space.'

'I had a long talk with your stepfather today,' Bart said, glancing at Kelsey and then chewing on his lip. 'From what he told me, things are considerably more complicated than I'd expected. I can't tell you any more than that about it right now.'

'That's not fair,' Kelsey complained. 'I want to know what's going on. Here I was, looking forward to a lovely evening and now you're—you're treating me like some kind of a weevil!'

'I'm sorry,' Bart said, picking up her hand and patting it, absently. 'It's just that I find myself in a position that I don't like at all, and I have to decide how to deal with it before I get to that meeting.'

'You aren't going to be in any danger, are you?' Kelsey asked anxiously.

'No, of course not.' He looked down at Kelsey and smiled, but the smile did not reach his eyes. 'Don't look so worried, Kelsey. I can take care of myself.'

A few minutes later, Henry stopped the car in front

of Bart's house. Bart helped Kelsey out, and then gave her a perfunctory kiss. 'Don't wait up for me,' he said. 'I don't know how long this will take.'

'I certainly will wait up,' she replied defiantly. 'I won't be able to sleep a wink until you're back safe and sound.'

At that, Bart's expression finally softened a little. 'It's nice to have someone care that much about me,' he said. 'I'll see you later, then.'

Kelsey went inside, then down to Bart's room, where only yesterday she had spent the most carefree day of her life. Now she felt as if her entire body were one tight knot of anxiety. What kind of meeting was Bart going to, and why wouldn't he tell her about it? What had Donald told him? He had better not have talked Bart into doing something dangerous. She did not really trust Bart's statement that he wasn't going to be in any danger. He had been acting too strangely.

'I think I'll call Donald and find out what he told Bart,' Kelsey muttered to herself. He might as well find out right now that Bart meant a great deal to her and that she would much prefer that someone else should deal with any really threatening situations. She sat down on the edge of Bart's bed and dialled her parents' number. After only one ring, her mother answered.

'Hello, Mom,' Kelsey said. 'Is Donald there?'

'No. No, he isn't,' her mother answered, her voice sounding tense. 'I thought that perhaps you'd seen him, but when I called your apartment all I got was that blasted answering machine of yours.'

'I'm sorry,' Kelsey said. 'When did Donald leave? Did you two have a fight?'

'Good heavens, no!' her mother replied vehemently. 'He left for Los Angeles about noon, but he was very vague about where he was going. To see some people, was all that he'd tell me, and he said he'd be back quite late tonight.'

Kelsey frowned. That sounded very much as though Donald was involved in the same meeting as Bart tonight, in addition to having seen Bart this afternoon, but she didn't want to mention that and worry her mother even more. 'I'm sure he's OK, Mom,' she said comfortingly. 'You know how men like to be mysterious at times. It makes them feel really tough and macho.'

'Well, I'm not sure,' her mother said, sounding almost as if she were about to cry. 'He not only wouldn't tell me where he was going, but he was packing his service revolver. He didn't know that I saw it, but I did.'

CHAPTER NINE

KELSEY was glad that she was sitting down, for the room started to reel around her. She fought desperately to calm herself, lest she communicate her panic to her already frantic mother. 'There's probably some perfectly simple explanation,' she managed to say, in surprisingly placid tones. 'He just didn't want to worry you. Men are sometimes terribly dimwitted about that.'

'They certainly are,' her mother agreed. 'Would you mind if we don't tie up the phone? I'm still hoping he'll call and let me know what's going on, or at least tell me that he's all right.'

Fat chance of that, Kelsey thought wryly. To her mother she said, 'All right. But call me if you hear anything or if he comes home, will you? I want to be sure he's OK too.' She suddenly realised that her mother did not know where she was. 'Oh, by the way, Mom, I'm at Bart Malone's house and I'll probably be here until after midnight.'

'At Bart Malone's house?'

'Yes, we've become very good friends,' Kelsey replied. 'I'll tell you about it later.'

'Well, at least someone's having a nice evening,' her mother said drily as she took down the number Kelsey gave her.

'That's what you think,' Kelsey muttered, after her mother had hung up. She had hoped for some consolation and now she felt worse than ever. She put some Mozart on the stereo and tried to get interested in a book, but to no avail. Then she alternately paced around the room and flopped down to sit in a tense little ball on the bed or a chair. When, at eleven o'clock, the telephone rang, she nearly knocked over the bedside lamp in her haste to answer it.

'Donald's home,' her mother announced. 'I still don't know where he was, but I think he's been drinking a little more than usual. He isn't drunk, but I can smell it on his breath, and he looks like the cat that ate the canary.'

'Can I talk to him?' Kelsey asked.

'No, he's in the shower, but he said to tell you, and I quote, that Bart Malone's the greatest guy in the world. I have no idea why I was supposed to tell you that.'

'I'm not sure that I do either,' Kelsey said with a sigh. Perhaps Bart had told Donald that they were planning to get married, but that hardly seemed a topic that would have come up at a meeting where Donald had felt it necessary to be armed. 'Well, let me know if you find out anything more,' she said.

'I will,' her mother promised. 'Will you be home tomorrow?'

'During the day,' Kelsey replied, 'but I'm going to the ballet with Bart tomorrow night.'

'That sounds nice,' said her mother. 'If I don't talk to you before then, have a good time.'

I'd rather have a good time right now and have Bart come home, Kelsey thought, after she had said goodnight to her mother. Why wasn't Bart home? He probably had a much shorter distance to travel than Donald did, unless the meeting had been half-way to Santa Barbara. She was just heading for the living-room to peer out of the front windows when she heard the door open. Seconds later she heard the sound of Bart whistling a melody from *Don Giovanni*.

'Well, aren't you jolly?' she said at the sight of him coming towards her, a silly grin on his face.

'I'm probably the jolliest person you'll ever meet, next to Santa Claus,' Bart said, picking her up and whirling her around. 'Whoops!' he said as his feet became tangled and he almost fell.

'You've been drinking,' Kelsey said accusingly. 'You'd better put me down before you fall down.'

Bart roared with laughter and swept Kelsey into his arms instead. 'Hey, it's almost like being married already. Come home a little drunk and the little woman points her finger at you and says naughty, naughty! But I like it. It sure beats coming home to an empty house and an empty bed.' He swerved into the bedroom and deposited Kelsey on his bed. 'See? Now my bed's not empty.'

'No, but your head is,' Kelsey said crossly. 'And in the morning it's going to feel like you've got two of them.'

'You're right. Absolutely right,' Bart agreed, beginning to fling his clothes off right and left. 'Come on, little love, take your clothes off and let's get into bed and make some whoopee.'

'You can go and get into a cold shower,' Kelsey snapped. 'I am definitely not in the mood. I think I'll go and sleep upstairs.'

'Aw, c'mon,' Bart said, frowning sulkily. 'Aren't you glad to have me back, safe and sound?'

'Of course I am,' Kelsey said. 'Very glad.' She sighed and then started to undress.

'That's my Kelsey,' Bart said, leaning over to kiss her warmly. 'You're going to get a good night's sleep, anyway. I'm too drunk to do anything else. I haven't been this drunk in years.'

'I'm glad to hear you don't make a habit of it,' Kelsey

said, shaking her head. Her heart began to melt, as Bart struggled with a shoelace and then looked at her hopefully. He was ridiculous, but as adorable as a huge, clumsy puppy. 'Here, let me,' she said, stooping to untie the knot. 'That must have been some meeting.'

'Best meeting I ever went to,' Bart agreed. 'Gotta have more like it.'

Not if I can help it, Kelsey thought grimly. She helped Bart out of the rest of his clothes, trying to ignore his foolish grin and his frequent attempts to kiss her. When he was undressed, she flung back the bedcovers. 'Get in there,' she ordered. He lay down, still smiling, apparently happy to have Kelsey tuck him in like a small child. She leaned over and kissed his lips. 'I certainly hope you're in better shape in the morning,' she said.

'I'll be in perfect shape,' Bart promised. 'Hey, we gotta go to the ballet tomorrow night and shoot some ducks.'

'Shoot ducks?'

'I mean swans,' Bart said. 'That's it, swans. Four little swans. Bang, bang, bang, bang.'

'You,' Kelsey said, 'are crazy.'

'I know it,' Bart said happily. 'G'night.'

Seconds later, he was sound asleep, leaving Kelsey still staring at him, shaking her head. Her mother had said that Donald looked like the cat who ate the canary, and Bart had had a very similar aura about him. What on earth could those men have been up to? Tomorrow, she was going to find out or die trying.

But, in the morning, Bart was no more forthcoming about his mysterious meeting than he had been the night before. 'You'll find out soon enough,' was all that he would say.

'Just for that, I hope that your hangover hangs

around all day,' Kelsey groused. She watched, as Bart downed a third cup of coffee and then rubbed his forehead and groaned. 'Serves you right,' she said unsympathetically.

'I know it,' Bart replied, shooting a dark look at Kelsey. 'I deserve every bit of it, and please don't get the idea that I make such an ass of myself very often. I'll be OK in a little while. Damn! We have to go to that ballet tonight, don't we?'

'I believe so,' Kelsey replied. She smiled wryly. 'If you can remember, would you please tell me why you said last night that you had to go and shoot four swans?'

'Oh, that!' Bart grinned. 'To relieve the boredom, I sometimes pretend I'm picking off the little swans from a duck blind as they dance by.'

'If you hate ballet so much, why go?' Kelsey asked. 'Why be a sponsor, or whatever?'

'I don't hate it. I'm just tired of *Swan Lake*,' Bart replied. 'It seems as if they close the season with it every year. Oh, by the way, my parents are going to stop by for a light dinner on the terrace before we go. I refuse to go to some blasted cocktail party beforehand and spend the entire evening starving for some real food.'

'That's . . . nice,' Kelsey said, although the idea of confronting his mother again, especially now that she really did plan to marry Bart, sent a shiver of nervousness through her. 'Are you planning to tell your parents . . . about us?' she asked hesitantly.

Bart shook his head. 'That announcement deserves a special occasion of its own.'

'Do you mean that you plan to wait until after we're married to tell them?' Kelsey demanded. 'Are you that worried about what your mother will think?'

'Of course not.' Bart looked at his watch. 'We'd better get going,' he said, leaving Kelsey to wonder which question he had answered.

It was only a little after nine a.m. when Bart dropped Kelsey and Henry off at her apartment. He kissed Kelsey lingeringly, but it was still not quite the passionate kiss that she longed for. Still, she thought, she should realise that every kiss he gave her could not be like those of that miraculous night and day they had spent making love. Bart was a busy man, with a lot on his mind, and she should be getting a few other things back on her mind, too. Even if they did get married at Las Vegas, she would still have her school term to finish, and she had a book to complete besides.

In spite of Bart's aversion to the ballet, Kelsey was looking forward to being able to wear one of the elegant gowns she had bought and had, so far, worn only once. The black chiffon with silver threads and the black-dyed Persian lamb jacket should be enough to set Bart's mother wondering where on earth she got the money to afford such things.

She went into her bedroom and took out her formal gown, inspecting it carefully to make sure there were no flaws or wrinkles. After that, she took a cup of coffee into her study, determined to get her mind on something constructive. She took out her manuscript of *The Case of the Crooked Claims* and tried to go over what she had written so far. Her brain refused to co-operate. When, for the third time, she found herself staring dreamily into space, trying to imagine what it would be like being married to Bart, she went into the kitchen, poured herself a fresh cup of coffee, and flopped restlessly down on a chair. 'I don't think I'm going to get much done today,' she said to Henry, who was deeply engrossed in reading the newspaper.

Henry looked up at Kelsey and smiled. 'Some days are like that, aren't they? Here, have part of the paper to read.' He handed a section of the morning paper to Kelsey.

'Might as well,' she said with a sigh. 'It's that or watch soap operas on TV.' Henry had given her the local news section, and she scanned through it methodically, scarcely registering what she was reading until an item in the top right-hand corner of the second page caught her eye. 'Victim Drops Suit' was the small headline. Robert Santos, the item reported, had dropped his lawsuit against the Big Winner supermarkets. It was rumoured there was a large out-of-court settlement, but neither he nor his lawyer could be reached for comment. Bart Malone, General Manager of the stores, refused to confirm or deny the rumours.

'I wonder why he didn't tell me about that?' Kelsey said, frowning.

'About what, Miss Kelsey?' Henry asked.

'One of the people who was suing the store,' she replied. 'The last one, Robert Santos. He dropped his suit. Hmmmm. That's really odd. It almost looked as if he had a legitimate claim, losing a finger and all.'

'I wouldn't know anything about it, miss,' Henry said, shaking his head and retreating behind his newspaper again.

Kelsey eyed him speculatively. Henry had driven Bart to the meeting last night. He would at least know where it had been, and he might have seen some of the other participants. 'I wonder if Robert Santos was at that meeting last night,' she mused aloud. 'Did you happen to see any of the people who went in?'

'I'm not at liberty to say anything about it,' Henry said, lowering his paper again and giving Kelsey a severe look.

'I was afraid of that,' Kelsey said resignedly. She turned her attention back to the newspaper. 'There's certainly not much information about the Santos case in the newspaper. Hardly worth reporting.' She chewed fretfully on her finger. Had another person got away with bilking the Big Winner stores out of some money, this time a large amount? Did that have anything to do with last night's mysterious meeting? How was Donald involved? Where did Ford Malone fit into the picture? Was there some link to organised crime? Drat! Kelsey drummed her fingers on the table in frustration. Here she sat, excluded from everything, guarded like someone's pet hamster. Well, she wasn't going to sit still for it! She was going to find out at least part of what was going on, and maybe all of it. Unless she was mistaken, young Mr Santos would know quite a bit, and she knew just where to find him. She jumped to her feet. 'Henry,' she announced, 'get your coat. We're going for a drive.'

'If you'll tell me where you want to go, I'll drive, Miss Kelsey,' Henry said as Kelsey got into the driver's seat of her car.

'No, thank you,' Kelsey said. 'I know where I'm going.' And, she thought to herself, Henry would probably baulk at going to Robert Santos' house. She had gathered long ago that he and Bart had very few secrets from each other. If Santos was involved at all in the things that were being kept from her, Henry probably knew about it and had instructions to make sure that she had no contact with the man.

The drive to Robert Santos' house seemed to Kelsey considerably shorter than it had when she had had to stop long enough for Bart to buy an old car. In only half an hour she turned on to the familiar street and had to pretend to cough loudly to cover the gasp at what she saw there. For, parked directly in front of Robert Santos' little house, was Ford Malone's red Maserati! She heard Henry's gasp as she pulled in and parked in front of the red sports car.

'Miss Kelsey, I don't think we ought to stop here,' Henry said, his voice trembling.

Kelsey glanced over at him. So he did know something. Well, she was not sure she should stop, either, now that she had seen Ford Malone's car, but her curiosity was so rampant and her adrenalin rushing so fast at the thought of confronting Ford Malone *in flagrante delicto*, that she could not bring herself to turn away.

'I have to,' she said. 'Don't worry, I'll be careful. But you might move over to the driver's seat in case we want to leave in a hurry.' Without looking further at Henry's horrified face, Kelsey got quietly out of her car and started towards the front door of Robert Santos' house, her heart pounding.

One fact immediately struck her as curious. There were no longer any toys lying about the garden, which was as bare as if the house were unoccupied. Perhaps, she thought, the Santos family had already moved to greener pastures in anticipation of their ill-gotten gains. But there was someone in the house. She could hear the sounds of male voices through the door. The voices were apparently coming from the kitchen at the back of the house, for Kelsey could see no one when she peered cautiously into the now bare living-room. If she were only a little closer, she would be able to hear what they were saying without being seen.

Carefully, Kelsey crept round the side of the house, keeping crouched well below the height of the windows. When she reached the back corner of the

house and peered around, she could see that Robert
Santos had an old pick-up van parked just outside the
back door. It was piled with furniture and boxes. As
she watched, the back door started to open and she
drew back round the corner, holding her breath and
listening intently.

'That's the last box,' Robert Santos was saying. His
words were followed by the thump of an object landing
in the van.

'I don't know how to thank you and your family for
your help,' said Ford Malone's voice.

'No problem,' replied the voice of Robert Santos.
'I've always wanted to take part in a scam like this
one.'

Good lord! Kelsey felt a sudden wave of dizziness.
They were talking about it in the open, just as brazenly
as you please! She clenched her hands tightly and
listened even more intently.

'It's not going to be easy, starting all over, even with
plenty of money,' Ford Malone said.

'I know, but it beats getting farther and farther in
the hole with no hope of ever getting out,' Robert
Santos replied. 'I sure wish I could stick around for
that party at Las Vegas on Friday night so I could
thank Kelsey Cameron in person. That's going to be
some bash.'

Party? Thank Kelsey Cameron? Kelsey's mind felt
as if it would explode from the wild churning that
began inside. That didn't make any sense! At least not
from her original set of premises.

Ford Malone chuckled. 'It should be fascinating. I
just hope Bart gets his part of the act together in time.'

'I think he will,' Robert Santos said. 'You should
have seen him come flying across the street when that
bunch of hoods started messing around by her car.

You be sure she knows that I'm getting along just fine, won't you? I could see she was really worried about me. Did you say that she still hasn't caught on that you all know that she and Joe Rocco are really the same person?'

'According to Bart and old Donald M., she hasn't the foggiest,' Ford Malone replied with another chuckle.

At the sound of those words, Kelsey bent and slunk off to the front of the house. She could not have stood up straight if she had wanted to. She felt as if she had been punched, right in the stomach. She got silently into her car, and looked at Henry. He was now sitting in the driver's seat, staring straight ahead, his face ghostly pale. 'Let's go home,' she said in an almost inaudible voice. 'I have a lot of thinking to do.'

But first, Kelsey thought, as Henry muttered a hoarse 'Yes, ma'am' and started the car, she would have to decide between various powerful, conflicting emotions. The first made her feel as if she might become violently ill, the second inclined her to take to her bed and cry her eyes out. The third, which she thought was probably the strongest and most practical, sent spurts of fiery rage through her, along with a chillingly cold anger that was already calculating how many of the apparent conspirators in the plot against her she could pick off with a high-powered rifle before anyone could stop her.

The conspirators. Who were they and why had they done it? Why, in heaven's name, would a group of men want to make a fool of her, make her think she was working on a real case, just because she wrote detective stories under an assumed name? Apparently they had paid Robert Santos a large sum of money to deceive her. Why? No hypothesis of any kind popped into

Kelsey's mind for that mystery, so she went back to the first question. Who?

She knew from what she had heard that Ford Malone, Robert Santos, and Bart were in on it. Bart, the man she had thought she loved. Not to mention her own stepfather, who was doubtless the Donald M. who Ford had mentioned. A man whom she had always trusted implicitly. Henry knew too, that was obvious, although he had no idea what she might have overheard. Best to keep it that way until she decided what to do. Who else? Her mother? Kelsey doubted that. Morris Carter? Possibly. Bart's mother? No, Kelsey decided after a moment's reflection, she was not one of them. Not the right type of person. And not a male. This smelled, from start to finish, like some kind of attempt by a group of males to put an uppity female in her place. She hadn't thought Donald would stoop to such a trick, although she knew he was not too keen on women as real detectives. Could there be any other men she had not thought of? Possibly Bart's father. Donald still saw him and described him as 'a lot of fun'. Maybe he was the one who had led Donald astray.

At that point Henry guided Kelsey's car to a stop in front of her apartment and looked over at her questioningly. 'Are you all right, Miss Kelsey?' he asked. 'You've been awfully quiet.'

Kelsey eyed him thoughtfully. No, she decided, she was not going to let on yet that she had the slightest idea that the whole story of the phoney lawsuits was even more phoney itself. 'I'm fine,' she said, giving him a little smile. 'It was just a bit of a shock to see those two men talking together in broad daylight, just as if there were nothing illicit going on. It's amazing, how some people have no conscience at all, isn't it?'

'It certainly is,' Henry agreed fervently.

Aha! Kelsey thought. I fooled him. He thinks they still have *me* fooled. Which, in a way, they did. There had to be more behind such an elaborate trick than a desire to prove that it could be done.

As soon as they were inside Kelsey's apartment, she went into her study, locked the door behind her, and sat down at her desk. Her mind was crystal-clear now, although her body was actually trembling with anger. Well, it could just stop, she thought grimly. She wasn't going to eat, or drink, or do anything else until she had figured out exactly what was going on and why. First of all, she needed to write down what she knew had happened, starting at the very beginning, just as she did with her novels. She took out a piece of paper and numbered down the side from one to ten.

Number One: Bart's letter to her, requesting the help of Joe Rocco.

That snake. He must have already known who she was. Did Donald tell him? If so, why? She had no idea. But, apparently, Bart was chosen to make the first move, to see if she could be trapped into going along with the trick. She had certainly fallen for that like a ton of bricks. With Donald's encouragement. Fallen. In the store, at Bart's feet. And soon, into his arms . . . and his bed! Had he told everyone about *that* last night, at what was obviously more of a party than a meeting? No, he couldn't have. Donald was there and he would not have approved, not have gone home looking smug. Or would he? Was there some sinister defect in her stepfather that she had failed to see before?

Number Two: Morris Carter's appearance at the hospital.

Bart's reaction to her marriage threat showed clearly

that he knew Carter was in on it. He had to be, in case
she contacted him. But her own accident was a
surprise. Doubtless Carter was told as soon as she was
in the ambulance. Her improvisation about marrying
Bart must have thrown them all into a fit. It certainly
confused Bart at the time.

Number Three: her visit to Robert Santos.

She had thought that it was her idea, but she had
been set up so beautifully. She had seen an actual
'victim'. What, she wondered, would have happened
if she'd wanted to see one of the others on the list?
Had they actually hired that many people to take part?
It was possible. Money was no object with those
people. Think of Bart stopping to 'buy' that car. Of
course, he had probably bought it earlier and left it
there at the gas station so that he could look as if he
were actually improvising as he went along. Were
those boys who accosted her a set-up, too? She
wouldn't be surprised. It gave Bart a wonderful excuse
to look heroic. Big man saves poor, fragile little
woman.

Number Four: Bart's exit on Friday night.

Maybe that was genuine. Maybe he was beginning
to have second thoughts about taking part in the trick.
He had seemed to enjoy that kiss. He would have had
to be dead not to, the way she flung herself at him.
How embarrassing.

Number Five: Ford Malone's appearance on
Saturday morning.

That one was hard to evaluate. The only thing that
Kelsey was sure of now was that he had not really been
there to threaten her after all. Too bad she hadn't
trapped his fingers in the door. He would probably
have confessed the whole scheme right then and there
if she had.

Number Six: Bart's note and reappearance on Sunday night.

The rest of the conspirators must have persuaded him to get back into the game. After all, with so much ingenuity and money already invested, they would hate it to end ahead of schedule. How clever to make her think she was really in danger, by having someone pretend to try to break into her apartment!

Number Seven: Bart's mother's appearance.

She was not part of the plan, Kelsey was sure. Poor woman, actually thinking that Bart was about to marry beneath his social class. Kelsey wrinkled her nose at the thought. If Bart hadn't turned out to be such a snake, it would have been fun to make Mrs Malone eat her words.

Number Eight: the ridiculous plan to 'Keep Kelsey Safe'.

It was really more a plan to keep her out of mischief until the denouement at Las Vegas, whatever that was supposed to be. It hadn't been such a bad experience, staying at Bart's lovely home, except for the fact that her heart had been broken in the process. He had been so convincing, so passionate. And, no doubt, he had had a wonderful time! No wonder he hadn't wanted to tell his parents that they were going to be married. It would be hard to sue him for breach of contract when it was her word against his!

'I will never again let myself fall in love,' Kelsey muttered to herself. 'Never! I will stay an unmarried schoolteacher until hell freezes over or I die, whichever comes first!'

Number Nine: the second trip to Robert Santos' house.

That had certainly been a bit of serendipity, reading that item in the newspaper, and then getting there just before he drove off, never to return, and finding Ford Malone there talking to him as she had. Had someone planted that item in the paper, or had there actually been a suit filed and then withdrawn in case she checked that out? It must have been the latter, because it couldn't have been certain that she would see the newspaper item.

Number Ten: the discovery that Robert Santos and everyone else in the plot knew that she and Joe Rocco were one and the same. That item spoke for itself. She had been betrayed!

Kelsey added Number Eleven: Ford Malone had said he hoped that Bart got his part of the act together. Santos thought that he would. Was Bart scheduled to make another daring but phoney rescue to impress her, perhaps before they all jumped out at her and yelled 'Surprise!' at the big party?

Kelsey shook her head and sighed. She went over and over the list, trying to make some sense of it. All the items were perfectly objective and true, but the only thread that held them all together was the fact that they contributed to an elaborate deception designed to make her think that she was taking part in the solution of a plot against the Big Winner supermarkets. Why?

Kelsey jabbed the paper so fiercely with her pencil as she made the question mark that the lead broke. Why would anyone want to treat her like that? What had she ever done? And why, oh, why, had she fallen so hopelessly in love with Bart Malone? She put her head down on her arms and burst into silent, racking sobs.

CHAPTER TEN

IT TOOK all Kelsey's ingenuity to repair the damage to her face that a long bout of crying produced. Her nose was red and her eyes were swollen and she had to pretend to Henry that a box containing mothballs, that she had opened in hopes of finding something she had stored away, had caused a violent allergic reaction. By five o'clock, when Bart arrived, aspirin, bags of ice and a skilful make-up job had restored her appearance to normal. Or maybe even better than normal, Kelsey thought, considering the appreciative way that Bart looked at her. She smiled at him and hoped fervently that she could find the inner strength to keep smiling until tomorrow night, even though her heart felt like a great leaden weight in her chest. For, during her long session of utter misery, she had given up any hope of understanding what had motivated the terrible deception against her, and decided to play the game out to the end. After that, she would decide what to do to get even. Right now, the idea of suing for enough to build herself a house even more elegant than Bart's sounded quite appealing.

Kelsey passed up the nightly swimming ritual, pleading that she didn't want to have to do her hair again. In reality, she did not want to have to look at Bart's long, sleek body, knifing through the water with graceful, sensual precision. She stayed well away from the windows, attending to her appearance with meticulous detail. Even her toenails had not the slightest chip in their magenta polish, her sheer stockings not the tiniest snag. She waited until she heard, at the front of the house, the sounds of people arriving and being invited out to the terrace. Then she drifted down the stairs and out on to the terrace herself. It was, she thought quite smugly, the entrance of her lifetime.

Bart stared at her as if he had never seen her before. Raymond Malone stood, open-mouthed, blinking in disbelief. Olivia Malone dropped her beaded evening bag and turned quite pale. When Bart at last recovered enough to come to her side, Kelsey smiled adoringly up at him. 'My goodness, but you look handsome tonight,' she said. 'I'll be the envy of every woman at the ballet.'

'And Bart will be the envy of every man,' Raymond Malone said gallantly, recovering his power of speech before his son did. He came towards Kelsey, his hand outstretched. 'I'm Raymond Malone, Kelsey,' he said. 'Your stepfather and I are old friends.'

'So he's told me,' Kelsey replied, shaking his hand and giving him a warm smile. It was, she thought bitterly, impossible not to smile at him, his own greeting seemed so geniunely friendly and kind.

'You look stunning, my dear,' Olivia Malone said, looking Kelsey over quite openly. 'Absolutely stunning.'

'Absolutely gorgeous,' Bart said, finally able to speak. 'Breathtaking.'

'Thank you . . . very much,' Kelsey said, feeling rather guilty in the light of the black thoughts she had been having about those who were praising her with such sincere warmth.

The rest of the evening went pleasantly enough, too. Bart fidgeted so much through the ballet that Kelsey began to feel almost sorry for him. He was much too tall to be comfortable in the seats, even though they were the best in the house. The ballet was far from over when he leaned over and whispered in her ear, 'Come on, let's get out of here. I've done my duty.'

Kelsey felt a shiver of fear. She was not sure whether it was because it was a strange time to leave and she didn't trust Bart any more, or because she didn't trust herself to be alone with him. She had not been lying when she said that he looked handsome in his dinner jacket. He looked so incredibly desirable that she felt as if her whole body were one giant ache of tension and longing.

They slipped out between the curtains at the back of the box and made their way down the curving staircase and out of the doors. Bart heaved a sigh of relief. 'That's over for another year,' he said, grinning as Kelsey gave him a reproving frown. 'I can't help it,' he said, 'if that's the way I feel. Would you like to go somewhere for a drink? We're not due at the sponsors' party for another hour.'

'Do we have to go?' Kelsey asked tightly. There would be dancing, she knew, and the idea of being in Bart's arms, knowing what she now knew, was more than she could bear.

'Well, I'm supposed to put in an appearance,' Bart said. 'I am one of the sponsors.'

'Then I'll have Henry take me home,' Kelsey said. 'I have a headache.'

'A headache?' Bart looked suspicious. 'Are you sure you aren't avoiding the party because of my mother? Because if that's it . . .'

'Certainly not!' Kelsey denied, a little too hotly. She did not want to argue, she only wanted to get away from Bart. Suddenly it seemed that every second she spent in his company was a kind of fiendish torture.

If only she could go back to her own little apartment, her own bed, her own cat for company, it would be heaven. But since she apparently had to hang on for one more day to find out what was going on, she was going to hang on! 'What do I have to do to make Henry appear?' she demanded. 'I want to go home right now!'

Bart looked at her strangely, but he spoke to the doorman and in a few minutes Henry and the limousine appeared in the drive. Kelsey got in without a word, then frowned as Bart got in beside her. 'You don't need to come,' she said coldly. 'I'm just going home and going to bed. Besides, won't your mother be upset if you don't stay for the party?'

'My mother was born upset,' Bart growled. 'Are you sure you're all right? You've seemed on edge all evening.' He leaned over and peered into Kelsey's face.

'I'm fine. Except for my headache,' she replied, staring straight ahead. 'I do wish you'd stayed.'

'If I'd wanted to, I would have,' Bart said calmly. 'Don't nag.'

'I'm not nagging,' Kelsey snapped. 'I never nag.'

'Could have fooled me,' Bart said.

He fell silent, and Kelsey said nothing either, all the way back to his house. Once inside, she paused and said formally, 'Thank you for a lovely evening. I'm going to sleep upstairs tonight, so I'll see you in the morning. Could you tell me what I'll need for the trip to Las Vegas? I really don't know quite what to expect there.'

Bart stared at her. 'Sleep upstairs?'

'Just this one last time,' Kelsey said, patting his arm. 'I really need my beauty sleep so I won't disappoint you tomorrow. It's going to be so exciting, going to Las Vegas with you. Getting married. Now, about what I should take?'

'Anything you like,' Bart replied, looking desperate. 'Kelsey, you're acting very strange. Are you sure you're all right? That it's only a headache? Because if you're ill, I can get a doctor out here . . .'

'I'm fine,' Kelsey interrupted. 'Don't you know that all brides get an attack of nerves beforehand? Just leave me alone. I'll be all right.' And if you don't, pretty soon, I'm going to fall apart! she thought.

Bart looked unconvinced, but he nodded. 'All right, but it's going to be awfully lonesome in that big bed without you.'

He smiled at Kelsey so wistfully that she almost felt guilty. If she thought for one minute that he really loved her . . . She clenched her hands tightly to strengthen her resolve. 'Just think of all the years and years ahead,' she said, as lightly as she could. When I won't be there either, she added to herself.

'I don't think that will help much,' Bart said drily. He followed as Kelsey crossed the long living-room to the stairs that led to her room.

'Well, goodnight,' Kelsey said, pausing with one foot on the first stair. 'What time should I set my alarm for?'

'I'm damned if you're going to bed without even kissing me,' Bart growled, ignoring her question. He pulled her roughly into his arms and tilted her chin up with one hand, his eyes searching frantically around her face, as if he was trying to discover why she was behaving so strangely. 'I love you, Kelsey,' he rasped. 'I know it's all happened terribly fast and there are some things that we still haven't had time to discuss but, believe me, we're going to have a wonderful life together. I—I shouldn't tell you this, but there's going to be a little surprise for you in Las Vegas. If everything works out, I know you're going to love it.'

Good lord, Kelsey thought, tears coming to her eyes. What kind of perverse logic could make Bart think she was going to love the surprise she already knew was awaiting her? She managed a wavering smile in order to pretend that her tears represented happiness. 'That sounds wonderful,' she choked out hoarsely. 'I'm going to have a surprise for you, too.'

Bart smiled crookedly. 'How sweet you are to have thought of something like that . . . whatever it is.'

He lowered his mouth to Kelsey's then, and in spite of everything she found herself responding to the depth of passion in his kiss and wondering dazedly if perhaps she should marry him just to be able to feel this way for a few minutes each day. When at last Bart raised his head, Kelsey felt as if her heart would break at the adoring softness of his beautiful grey eyes.

'I think that now I may be able to survive the night,' he said softly. 'I want to leave as early as possible, so you can have Henry run you home to pack right after breakfast, and I'll pick you up there at about eleven o'clock. That will give me time to finish making my arrangements to be away for a while. Maybe we'll decide to stay for longer than two days.'

Kelsey stared at him, wondering if she would be physically torn in two by the conflicting emotions that she felt. She wanted so desperately to believe in him. But how could she? 'I—I'll be ready,' she said, and fled upstairs to her room.

There were two things that Kelsey always remembered when she thought about the following day. First was the fact that she could remember scarcely anything about the part of the day before they got to the famous hotel and casino in Las Vegas where Bart had made reservations. She knew that she had gone home and packed in a sort of trance. She put on a black satin camisole-dress with a matching jacket. Black, she thought, was suitable for the occasion.

While she and Bart were driving to Las Vegas, she stayed in a kind of suspended animation. It felt as bizarre as one of those out-of-body experiences reported by people who had supposedly been pronounced dead and were then revived. She seemed to be watching herself watching Bart, to see if he gave away any clue that their trip was for anything but their own pleasure. The only clue that he did give was hard to interpret. He acted almost perfectly normally, but he was pale, and when he was not speaking he clenched his jaw so hard that the muscles in his cheeks stood out in hard ridges.

The second thing that Kelsey remembered, even before the action began, was that as soon as she stepped out of Bart's car her senses suddenly snapped into incredibly sharp focus. She seemed able to see almost three hundred and sixty degrees around her, and she could hear the smallest whisper from a familiar voice, even in the noise of the crowded hotel. She also remembered wondering to herself if that kind of response was what made it possible for real detectives to stay alive.

They had not even gone to the reception desk when Kelsey heard Donald's voice say, 'There are Bart and Kelsey now.'

Kelsey turned and saw, about twenty feet away, her stepfather and Raymond Malone standing at the door to one of the casino rooms. Apparently Bart was also hearing very well, for she felt him grasp her elbow and head directly towards the older men. She looked up, and saw that he looked more pale and grim than ever. As soon as they drew near Donald and Ray, she saw her stepfather raise his hand slightly and make a gesture that meant that something had gone well. A split second later, Bart's face relaxed and the colour began to return.

'Thank heaven,' he said softly. 'Where's Ford?'

'In the bar with the ladies,' Donald replied. 'We were just going to join them.' He looked at Kelsey. 'I expect you're surprised to find your mother and I are here. And Ray and Olivia too.'

'Not even slightly. I expected you to be,' Kelsey said, glancing coolly first at the two older men and then at Bart. 'You all aren't nearly as clever as you think you are. Did you and mother drive or fly?'

Donald's expression was caught between a smile and a frown as he looked from Kelsey to Bart for some explanation of her lack of surprise. 'Er . . . we flew,' he said. 'Thought we'd get here early and get in a little gambling before the evening show.'

'And it's going to be quite a show, isn't it?' Kelsey said, smiling sweetly first at Donald and then at Bart, who was looking at her with a peculiar, thoughtful intensity. She looped a hand through Bart's and Donald's elbows. 'Let's all go and have a drink and talk for a while, shall we? I don't feel like going up to our rooms just yet.' In fact, she had no intention of ever going to any room in this hotel! She was not going to sit around and wait to be taken somewhere where the results of whatever had made Bart so pale and anxious earlier could be sprung on her as a final insult. She had decided, during a long and sleepless night, that she was going to give everyone a good piece of her mind and then catch the first plane back to Los Angeles!

'You're certainly looking luscious,' Donald commented. 'That's quite a dress.'

'This little old thing from Giorgio's?' Kelsey purred. 'I'm glad you like it.' She steered the men towards the cocktail lounge area. She could feel Bart's breath on her cheek and hear him begin, 'Kelsey, how did . . .' when she saw Ford Malone, leaning against a golden post and talking to a leggy blonde in a mini-skirt. 'My goodness, look who's here,' Kelsey said. She dropped the men's arms and moved towards Ford, Bart now right at her side. She could feel his eyes looking at her as she held out her hand towards Ford Malone. 'Hello, Ford Malone, you handsome thing,' she said, beaming at the surprised man and holding out her hand. 'How nice to see you again. I was so glad to hear that Robert Santos didn't really lose his finger, but I do regret that I didn't get yours. If I'd known what you were up to, I wouldn't have bothered counting to three.'

Ford Malone gave Kelsey's hand a brief squeeze and then dropped it as if it were on fire. 'What's going on?' he asked, looking apprehensively at Bart. 'I thought . . .'

'So did I,' Bart interrupted. 'Kelsey, what is going on?'

'Going on?' Kelsey asked, widening her eyes and batting her eyelashes at him. 'Why, I'm just enjoying meeting old friends. Come on, let's join the others at their table. We do have so much to talk about.'

'Kelsey, I think maybe you and I had better have a talk,' Bart said, taking hold of her elbow.

'Don't touch me!' Kelsey snapped, glaring at him. 'You'll get your turn, along with everyone else.'

Bart's lips tightened into a grim line. 'Ford, maybe you'd better see if we can have that private room right now.'

'I think you're right,' Ford agreed, and disappeared quickly.

'What's the matter?' Kelsey asked, giving Bart a sulky pout. 'Are you afraid I'm going to make a scene? Why, I haven't even said hello to my mother and your mother yet.' She drifted over to where the two older couples were sitting at a round table almost surrounded by a soft lounge. 'Hello, Mother,' she said. 'Are you looking forward to the party?'

'Well, I . . .' Kelsey's mother looked quickly over at Donald. 'I guess so,' she finished. 'Actually, I didn't know there was going to be a party.' She looked at Olivia Malone. 'Did you?'

Mrs Malone shook her head. 'Ray didn't tell me about any. But then, he often forgets to tell me about things like that.' She smiled vaguely at her husband. 'Did you forget, dear?'

'Oh, I don't think he forgot,' Kelsey said, reaching for her mother's whisky sour and picking it up. 'You don't mind if I have some of this, do you? I think I'm going to need it. It's going to be a very unusual party. Sort of a barnyard affair, and I get to be the goat.'

'What in hell are you talking about?' Bart asked, taking hold of Kelsey's arm and pulling her next to him again.

'Maybe it's going to be more like charades, or Twenty Questions, or something like that,' Kelsey said, batting her eyelashes at Bart again, 'and then everyone can have a good laugh at my expense and get drunk. Is that right?' She flicked a glance from Bart, to his father, to Donald, and let her eyes rest on her stepfather, bitterly accusing. 'You snake in the grass!' she said. 'You must be the one who told. Why? What on earth did you hope to gain from making a fool of me?'

'Make a fool of you? That's the last thing in the world we plan to do!' Donald said quickly. 'I don't really see why you feel that way. After all, the secret's never going any farther than just the people here and a couple of others who are coming to the . . . the party.'

'I suppose that I should be glad it's not being broadcast live on national television,' Kelsey said icily. 'Or were you planning on having a television camera record my face on tape later, while you revealed your nasty little secrets, one by one? Well, I'm happy to tell you that you won't have an opportunity to do that, because, as you can plainly see, I found out all about what you were up to. The only thing I haven't figured out is *why* you did it? If you didn't plan to make a fool of me and prove that I'm not really any kind of a detective, what on earth was the point of such an elaborate scam? Don't you people have anything better to do with your time?'

Ford Malone reappeared at Bart's side. 'We can have the private room now,' he said in a low voice.

Bart nodded. 'Thanks. You all go on in. I need to talk to Kelsey alone first.'

'No, you don't, and the rest of you stay right here,' Kelsey said coldly, refusing to look at Bart. She was not going to let his sweet smile and soft, silvery eyes shake her resolve. So far, she seemed to be having things her way and she was enjoying it quite a lot, considering the pain that was behind it all.

When everyone stopped, staring at her, she went on, 'I have a few words to say to all of you and then I am going home. First of all, I can't imagine what possessed any of you to imagine that I would enjoy being deceived. Secondly,' she glared at Bart, 'I don't know why you pretended you didn't know I was Joe Rocco, or what you hoped to gain from taking part in this—this mess, but I can tell you right now that I'm not the prize. I wouldn't marry you if you were the last man on earth! Last, but not least, I hope that you all think very hard before you play games with someone's life again, because it's no fun for the victim. I'm not sure I'll ever be the same. And now I'm going home to my own nice apartment, my cat, and my writing. And,' she glared at Bart again, 'don't anyone dare try to stop me!'

With that, she whirled and ran across the lobby, the blinding tears that she had so rigidly held in check streaming down her face. 'Taxi?' she croaked hoarsely at the blurred image of the doorman.

'Right here, ma'am,' he said, opening a door for her. He shook his head sadly as the taxi sped away. How much, he wondered, had she lost?

'Take me to the airport,' Kelsey gasped. 'As fast as you can.'

'Yes, ma'am,' said the taxi-driver. He handed a box of Kleenex to her as he started off. 'You'd better try and dry up,' he said unsympathetically. 'The world ain't really gonna end.'

'I . . . know that,' Kelsey choked out, between attempts to dry her tears and blow her nose. 'But I feel like it is!' She began sobbing again. There was no feeling of triumph, no pleasure in what she had done. Everyone had looked so stunned, Bart and Donald especially. Why? How did they *think* she would feel?

'Tch, tch, tch!' clucked the taxi-driver. 'How much did y' lose?'

'It wasn't money,' Kelsey replied hoarsely. 'Who cares about money?' At the moment she would give every penny she had to wipe out the past week and start again.

'Some of us have to,' the taxi-driver said drily.

'I know that, too,' Kelsey said, sniffling vigorously. 'I'm just a schoolteacher. I meant, there are things that are more valuable than money. People.'

'Some of 'em,' the taxi-driver said. 'Uh-oh. What's this all about?' He slowed and pulled over to the side of the street.

'Why are you stopping?' Kelsey cried. 'I want to hurry!' She did not want to find that someone, Bart especially, had decided to come after her. Her anger had vanished. She felt only numb and lost and alone.

'Lady,' the taxi-driver said, looking to his left, 'when a limo with tinted bulletproof glass wants me to pull over, I pull over.'

Kelsey looked out and saw what the driver meant. An immensely long limousine had pulled up beside them, the dark windows revealing nothing of the occupants. She felt her heart accelerate even faster. Should she get out and start to run? The door opened, and Bart's familiar dark head emerged, followed by his tall, lanky form. 'Damn!' Kelsey cried. 'I don't want to talk to him now!' She was so confused that she had no idea how she felt about Bart or anything else. She desperately needed some time alone to think things through, but it seemed that she was not to get it.

'Shall I call the cops?' the driver asked calmly.

'No. No, of course not,' Kelsey replied. She could see Bart's face clearly again, see his anxious concern as he came towards the taxi and opened the door.

'Come on, Kelsey,' he said, holding out his hand to her. 'I'm not leaving, so you might as well come out. You've apparently got a lot of misconceptions that we need to straighten out. We'll get everything out in the open and go on from there.'

Kelsey stared at Bart's hand, and then at his face, so strong and serious, and at the same time gentle and understanding. She closed her eyes and nodded. 'All right. But I'm still not sure that I should believe you.'

'I understand,' Bart said. He smiled crookedly. 'At least I think I do.' As Kelsey swung her feet out of the taxi, he scooped her up into his arms. 'Just remember that I love you,' he said, dropping a kiss on her forehead. 'That's what really matters.'

He opened the door of the limousine and helped her in. 'Kelsey, meet Bennett, my parents' chauffeur,' he said, getting in beside her. 'Just drive around for a while, Ben,' he said. He put his arm around Kelsey, who was sitting rigidly, staring straight ahead. 'Look at me, Kelsey,' he said firmly, taking his hand and turning her face towards him.

'This had better . . .' Kelsey began, trying desperately to maintain at least a little resentment in the face of Bart's loving but worried gaze. He put his finger to her lips and silenced her.

'Before you say anything,' he said, 'there is something that I want you to know. At the beginning of all this, I had no idea that you were really Joe Rocco. I didn't know it until Wednesday, when Donald decided that I'd better be told the whole story. As far as I know, only he and Ray and Ford and Robert Santos, and a couple of FBI agents whom you'll meet soon, know, and none of us will tell, so please stop worrying about that. OK?' Bart lowered his hand slowly, his eyes anxiously on Kelsey's.

'FBI agents?' Kelsey stared at Bart, a sick little knot beginning in her stomach. 'What does the Federal Bureau of Investigation have to do with any of this?'

'They got involved when Ford discovered the connection between the supposed accident victims, the insurance claims adjuster and a mobster named Willie "The Widget" Bascomb who hangs around Las Vegas. Ford talked Santos, who, by the way, *did* lose a finger, into turning state's evidence and actually wearing a wire when he made a delivery to Bascomb this morning. He could have been in considerable danger. That's why I was so tense this morning, but it all went well. Santos is now under the witness protection programme, so he won't be coming to the party in your honour.'

'In . . . my honour?' Kelsey croaked out hoarsely. All of a sudden, all her logic seemed to have fallen completely apart.

'That's right. You were the one who had the original idea of how the whole insurance scam might operate. Donald said that you'd talked it over with him a couple of months ago for a book you were writing. He passed it along to my father. Unbeknownst to me, Dad put Ford to work on it, and it turned out that you were exactly right. So, if everything worked out as we hoped that it would this morning, we planned, among other things, to have a surprise celebration in your honour this evening.'

Kelsey felt as if she would like to sink straight down through the floor of the limousine and disappear like a small pebble. 'Oh, gosh,' she whispered, 'I've been so stupid. I'm so sorry. It's just that when I heard Ford talking to Robert Santos it sounded like . . .'

'You heard what?' Bart interrupted, frowning. 'When?'

'Yesterday morning,' Kelsey replied. She explained about her trip to Robert Santos' house. 'And after you'd come home from that so-called meeting the night before, looking so smug, I just naturally assumed that the joke was on me. What on earth was that meeting about?'

'The first part of it was no joke,' Bart said with a grimace. 'It was a kind of sting operation to nail old Morris Carter, who had cleverly managed to slide out from under everything until then. I didn't like the idea, because I wasn't sure I could pull it off. I was so angry at what I'd found out from Donald that I wanted to throttle Carter, and instead I had to play the part of a wimpy jerk who practically begged him to stop the lawsuits.'

'If there's one thing you're not, it's a wimpy jerk,' Kelsey said, touching his cheek with her fingertips. 'Oh, Bart, I'm so sorry. I was so wrong about . . .'

Before she could finish, Bart pulled her into his arms and kissed her so passionately that Kelsey was breathless, her heart pounding with new-found happiness when he stopped. 'Don't ever again tell me that you wouldn't marry me if I were the last man on earth,' he scolded, silver sparks flashing as he looked into her eyes intently, 'and don't ever believe that I'd maliciously deceive you. I love you too much to ever want to hurt you.'

'I don't think I ever really believed it, deep in my heart,' Kelsey said. She buried her face against Bart's shoulder, unable to face the hurt she saw in his eyes. 'I'd give anything not to have been so stupid. Please forgive me. I do love you and I do want to marry you. If you'll still have me.'

'Of course I will!' Bart said gruffly. He kissed Kelsey again. She could feel the hard tension of his body finally relaxing until at last he raised his head and sighed deeply. His voice was soft and warm as he said, 'Now, all I want to do is take you somewhere and make love to you. Where was I?'

'The sting,' Kelsey murmured, snuggling against him. 'Did it work?'

'It did. I convinced Carter that I was desperate and asked if he could help since he said he could do anything for a price. He named the price, I gave him the money, and he was taken into custody. That, in a nutshell, describes the worst half-hour I've ever spent. I felt like I'd been through the proverbial wringer afterwards.'

'And, afterwards, everyone celebrated. A lot,' Kelsey said, looking up at him with a knowing smile.

'There was a lot to celebrate,' Bart said. He chuckled and gave Kelsey another quick kiss. 'Donald and my dad were feeling pretty pleased with themselves after I told them that we were planning to get married. I was angry with them, too, for thinking that they needed to meddle in my life, but since everything turned out so well I decided to relent.'

He laughed outright as Kelsey's eyes narrowed and she asked, 'What everything are you talking about?'

'Well, I suppose you've wondered how I happened to write that letter asking for Joe Rocco's help. It's not the sort of thing that I'd ordinarily do.'

'I think that I did get that right,' Kelsey replied. 'I figured that Donald had something to do with that, probably in league with your father. Donald all but told me to write the letter that I wrote back to you, although at the time he was so subtle that I didn't catch on. Did your father tell you to write to Joe Rocco about the accidents?'

'He suggested it, and then kept asking if I'd done it.' Bart's eyes now sparkled with silver shafts of mirth. 'You thought you'd been victimised by the accident scam but, in reality, we were both the victims of a pair of matchmaking men who somehow got the notion that you and I would make a good pair.' He laughed softly and gave Kelsey a hug. 'How right they were!'

'And that part I never even suspected,' Kelsey said with a groan. 'It must have been a pretty complicated scheme. Why didn't they just introduce us?'

'They didn't think that that would work. Apparently, it all started one afternoon when the two of them had a few drinks together at their shooting club. Dad was telling Donald about the string of accidents and how worried I was. Donald mentioned the ideas that you'd talked over with him. Then they got to talking about us. They thought that we had a lot in common and ought to meet. They thought of introducing us, but Dad was afraid that I'd just be my usual workaholic self, too busy to follow up, and Donald thought that you'd do your usual trick of backing off from any relationship with a man, as you'd been doing ever since Tom died. I'm not sure how it happened, but eventually it came out that I was a Joe Rocco fan, and then Donald spilt the beans about your pseudonym. From there, it was only a little jump for them to decide to try to bring us together in connection with the lawsuits, and see what happened. They thought that, if we had something to do, we might forget our personal quirks and get acquainted in spite of ourselves. I'll have to admit, it was pretty clever of them.'

'I'd say it was downright diabolical,' Kelsey said drily. 'That sneaky Donald! He flat-out denied it when I asked him if he'd let the cat out of the bag, but I guess that I can forgive him. I'm so glad you wrote that letter.'

'I guess I am, too,' Bart said with a rueful smile. 'I think it speeded up our courtship if nothing else.' He caressed Kelsey's cheek gently. 'Are you ready to go back to the hotel now and relieve some anxieties there?'

Kelsey nodded. 'I owe a lot of apologies. I hope that everyone's as willing to forgive me as you are.'

'I'm sure they will be,' Bart assured her. 'Besides,'

his eyes flashed with mischievous lights, 'there's still a surprise that I haven't told you about.'

'I'm not sure that I'm up to any more surprises,' Kelsey said with a sigh. 'Right now, I just want to curl up in your arms and pretend the rest of the world doesn't exist. But I'd better repair my make-up instead.'

By the time they were back at the hotel, Kelsey had done a reasonable job of repairing her tear-stained make-up. She felt her waning energy rekindled by the loving squeezes of Bart's arm round her shoulders and his frequent smiles, full of suppressed excitement.

'What are you up to now?' Kelsey demanded.

'You'll see,' replied Bart, smiling again.

They followed the hotel manager to one of the private meeting-rooms. The manager whispered something into Bart's ear and then left after Bart grinned and nodded. Then Bart opened the door and led Kelsey into a small meeting-room. It did not, Kelsey thought, look much like a party. There was a large oval table, around which sat Mr and Mrs Malone, Ford Malone and his blonde friend, Kelsey's mother and stepfather, Kelsey's sister and her husband, and two pleasant-looking men in dark suits. There was nothing on the table except pitchers of iced water and drinking-glasses.

Kelsey blushed as everyone burst into applause as she and Bart entered. Bart escorted Kelsey to the head of the table. 'May I present the heroine of the hour, Miss Kelsey Cameron,' he said. He bowed to her, then took a seat and left her standing before the group, who applauded enthusiastically once more.

'Thank you so much. I don't deserve this, after what I said,' she said, blinking back the tears of happiness that came to her eyes at the sight of their smiling faces. 'Maybe I should explain.' She looked pleadingly at

Bart. 'Would you help?'

'Anything for you,' he replied gallantly, and between them they quickly told the reason for Kelsey's mistaken conclusions.

'I'm afraid I was so desperate to solve some crime that I looked in the wrong places,' Kelsey concluded. 'I'm very grateful that everything turned out so well.'

'And we're grateful to you,' said Raymond Malone, 'for helping get the Big Winner stores back on the winning track.' He reached beneath the table and produced a large silver cup which he carried round the table to Kelsey. 'On behalf of everyone involved, we'd like to present you with this trophy which we will have suitably engraved to that great detective, Joe Rocco.' He bowed and handed the cup to Kelsey with a flourish.

'Speech!' called out Ford Malone.

Kelsey blinked back more happy tears. 'I'm afraid I haven't much to say,' she said, 'except thank you, and thank you all for coming here to do this for me. It's the nicest thing that's ever happened to Joe Rocco. He usually labours in obscurity.' She looked at Bart. 'Do you think we ought to . . . I mean, does everyone know about . . . us?'

Bart smiled. 'Yes, I think that information has been passed around, but we may as well make it official.' He stood up beside Kelsey and put his arm around her. 'Ladies and gentlemen, Kelsey and I have an announcement to make, and this seems like the ideal time. We plan to be married, as soon as possible.'

There was another round of applause. Kelsey noticed out of the corner of her eye that Donald left the room as if on cue, but she was so busy accepting congratulations from everyone else and hugging her mother and sister and even Olivia Malone that she had no time to ask Bart what Donald was up to. The two dark-suited men, the FBI agents Bart had mentioned, introduced themselves and congratulated Kelsey warmly. One of them produced a Joe Rocco book for Kelsey to autograph. Ford Malone gave Kelsey a resounding kiss and a hug.

'Sure glad you didn't get my fingers, sister-in-law,' he teased. 'I knew right away you could handle old Bart here.'

'Get your fingers?' Bart asked, eyeing his brother questioningly. 'What in the devil are you talking about?'

Ford explained about his visit to Kelsey. 'I was just checking her out,' he concluded with a rascally grin. 'I knew what Dad and Donald were up to, but I didn't know that she was Joe Rocco at the time, either, or I'd have been more careful.'

'And I thought that you were one of the bad guys,' Kelsey said, shaking her head. She looked up at Bart. 'You said you did, too, when you came over on Sunday and insisted on staying all night to protect me from him.'

'I did,' Bart said, grinning sheepishly as Ford roared with laughter.

'Hey, little brother,' said Ford, giving Bart's shoulder a friendly poke, 'that ploy's almost worthy of me. You knew damned well that I'd never hurt Kelsey. I only break hearts, not bones.'

'At the time I wasn't completely sure of that,' Bart replied. 'Besides, there were some other pretty ugly characters involved.'

'Hold on,' Kelsey interrupted. 'Talking of that, who was it who tried to break in to my place, then, that night? We thought it was you, Ford.'

'Not guilty.' Ford shrugged. 'The crime rate around

here is pretty high—it was probably just a routine attempt. I'm surprised it hasn't happened before; you've been lucky!'

'You see!' grinned Bart. 'You do need me around for some things.'

There was suddenly a sound from the end of the room. 'Close your eyes, Kelsey,' Ford ordered, and at the same moment Bart put his hand across Kelsey's face.

'Now what?' Kelsey demanded, listening to what sounded like a sliding door being opened.

'Come with me,' Bart said, carefully walking Kelsey ahead of him, her eyes still covered, towards the end of the room from which the sound had come. 'Now look,' he said, removing his hand.

Kelsey looked, and then let out a gasp. 'Oh, Bart! It's beautiful. Is it . . . for us?'

'Who else?' he asked, bending to kiss her on the cheek. 'Our very own wedding chapel.'

Tears of happiness ran unchecked down Kelsey's cheeks as she gazed at the room before her. The adjoining meeting-room had been turned into a wedding chapel overflowing with flowers. In the centre, a deep red carpet led to a gleaming white altar. Behind the altar stood a solemn-looking man in vestments. To the side, a grey-haired woman began playing softly on a small organ.

'How did you manage all of this?' Kelsey asked, dazed.

'Ford had seen this done before, so we called and they got it together in record time,' Bart replied. 'I hope you like it.' He raised his eyebrows questioningly.

Kelsey threw her arms around him and hugged him tightly. 'I love it,' she replied. 'It's the most absolutely perfect surprise I've ever seen. And everyone's here whom we'd want to have at our wedding. Bart Malone, you are a wonder.'

'Thank you, but Ford deserves a lot of the credit,' Bart said, smiling at her lovingly. 'And I think he has another little surprise for you.' He raised his head and called to his brother, 'Ford, bring Celia over.'

Ford came towards them, propelling his blonde friend beside him. 'This is Celia Johnston,' he said, introducing the blonde to Kelsey. 'She owns a bridal boutique in Beverly Hills, and she brought a few bridal gowns along for you to choose from. Just go along with Celia and she'll fix you up. Take your mother and sister with you to help.'

'I feel as if a nightmare had turned into a beautiful dream,' Kelsey said to her sister as they followed Celia down a hallway. 'Pinch me, Maggie, so that I know I'm really awake.'

'I'm not sure I am,' her sister admitted. 'We only found out this morning that we were coming to your wedding. But it looks to me as if you've found a wonderful man, and this is certainly the way to have a wedding. It took Mother months to get mine organised.'

'I hope you don't mind that it's so sudden?' Kelsey said, turning anxiously to her mother.

'Mind?' Mrs McMurphy smiled and shook her head. 'From what Donald told me, you're a very lucky woman. He thinks the world of Bart. Besides, time's flying. I need a few more grandchildren.'

Kelsey put her arm round her mother and hugged her. 'We don't plan to keep you waiting,' she said.

Among the bridal gowns that Celia had brought, Kelsey found one that suited her perfectly. As soon as she was dressed, the women returned to the chapel, where Bart now waited, wearing a white dinner jacket, with Ford at his side. The organist struck up 'Here Comes The Bride', and Donald came forward to escort Kelsey down the little aisle. He did look, Kelsey thought as she smiled at his ear-to-ear grin, as if he'd had a large dish of canary. At the altar she took Bart's hand and together they repeated their simple vows.

Later that night, when the celebration was over and Kelsey lay in Bart's arms, basking in the afterglow of his passionate love-making, he kissed her cheek softly and asked, 'Well, Miss Cameron, how does it feel to be Mrs Malone?'

'Heavenly,' she replied.

HARLEQUIN

Coming Next Month

#3067 ANOTHER MAN'S RING Angela Carson
Judi knows she doesn't want to marry Robert—but breaking it off won't be
easy. A job offer in Thailand provides an escape, until she realizes that
working for Nick Compton, she's jumped from the frying pan into the fire!

#3068 LOVE'S RANSOM Dana James
Zanthi enjoys her diplomatic post as assistant secretary on a small Caribbean
island—but she senses something very odd is happening. Especially when
surveyor Garran Crossley arrives and she is assigned to accompany him on his
land survey. . . .

#3069 THE TURQUOISE HEART Ellen James
Annie Brooke travels to New Mexico to restore a damaged painting for
Derrek Richards. A simple job, she thinks. But the feelings Derrek arouses in
Annie's heart are far from simple. . . .

#3070 A MATTER OF PRINCIPAL Leigh Michaels
Patrick's job is to sort out Camryn's finances—but he is threatening her whole
way of life. To protect herself and her young daughter, Camryn has to fight
him, though he proves difficult to resist—both as a banker and as a man!

#3071 HILLTOP TRYST Betty Neels
Oliver Latimer is safe and reassuring, and Beatrice is glad he was there to pick
up the pieces when her life turned upside down. Against Colin Ward's charm,
however, Oliver seems to have nothing to offer—until Beatrice takes a good
second look. . . .

#3072 A SUMMER KIND OF LOVE Shannon Waverly
Recently widowed, Joanna Ingalls needs a quiet summer alone with her five-
year-old son. But when they arrive at her father's cottage, she's shocked to
find Michael Malone living there—the man she'd loved so desperately six
years before.

Available in August wherever paperback books are sold, or through
Harlequin Reader Service:

In the U.S.
901 Fuhrmann Blvd.
P.O. Box 1397
Buffalo, N.Y. 14240-1397

In Canada
P.O. Box 603
Fort Erie, Ontario
L2A 5X3

HARLEQUIN
American Romance

THE LOVES OF A CENTURY...

Join American Romance in a nostalgic look back at the Twentieth Century—at the lives and loves of American men and women from the turn-of-the-century to the dawn of the year 2000.

Journey through the decades from the dance halls of the 1900s to the discos of the seventies ... from Glenn Miller to the Beatles ... from Valentino to Newman ... from corset to miniskirt ... from beau to Significant Other.

Relive the moments ... recapture the memories.

Look now for the CENTURY OF AMERICAN ROMANCE series in Harlequin American Romance. In one of the four American Romance titles appearing each month, for the next twelve months, we'll take you back to a decade of the Twentieth Century, where you'll relive the years and rekindle the romance of days gone by.

Don't miss a day of the CENTURY OF AMERICAN ROMANCE.

A CENTURY OF
AMERICAN ROMANCE
1900's

The women...the men...the passions...
the memories....

CAR-1

COMING SOON

In August, two worlds will collide in four very special romance titles. Somewhere between first meeting and happy ending, Dreamscape Romance will sweep you to the very edge of reality where everyday reason cannot conquer unlimited imagination—or the power of love. The timeless mysteries of reincarnation, telepathy, psychic visions and earthbound spirits intensify the modern lives and passion of ordinary men and women with an extraordinary alluring force.

Available next month!

EARTHBOUND—Rebecca Flanders
THIS TIME FOREVER—Margaret Chittenden
MOONSPELL—Regan Forest
PRINCE OF DREAMS—Carly Bishop